Heading Home

by

John Malone

For my father, Jack Malone, 1903-1991

John Malone

Manuscript consultant: Susan C. Snowden

Cover design: Keith Spaulding

ISBN 978-0-6151-5239-4

Riverman Press, Publisher
54 Chinquapin Lane
Waynesville, NC 28786

Preface

Last September I made a business trip to Pittsburgh, where my family lived for many years. The surviving members of the family all live elsewhere these days, but there is still a Malone burial plot with six graves in Homewood Cemetery in Pittsburgh's East End. Finding myself at loose ends on a warm autumn Sunday afternoon, I decided to visit it before catching my evening flight back home to the mountains of Western North Carolina.

The cemetery is a peaceful green oasis in the middle of the noisy city. It blankets a tree-shaded hilltop adjacent to Frick Park, criss-crossed with a complicated grid of access roads leading to its hundreds of graves, tombs and monuments. Fortunately I had a map giving directions to the final resting place of my family, or I would have become hopelessly lost, for it had been many years since I last visited those graves. Turning the rental car off Dallas Avenue, I drove through the main gate and swung left along the tall iron fence that separates the cemetery from the street. A short distance farther on, I found the way in to the family plot and parked the car.

Walking along the row of small headstones lined up in front of the massive, gray granite centerpiece, marked only with the word "MALONE," I stopped at the newest grave, that of my older sister Emily, a psychiatrist, who died of lung cancer in 1991. Right next to my sister's grave are the two oldest graves in our family plot, those of Thomas James Malone and his wife, Roxa Powell Malone. They were the first of my ancestors to come to Pittsburgh, arriving in 1880 with two small children from Antiquity, a tiny Ohio River village almost exactly midway between Pittsburgh and Cincinnati.

Tom's parents, Jack and Margaret Malone, crossed the sea from Ireland just before the Famine in 1842 and arrived in Brownsville, Pennsylvania, at that time a busy town at the crossing point of the old National Pike on the Monongahela River. In an effort to complete a family genealogy prepared by my father years earlier, I made several trips to Ireland starting in 1999 to find more information about Jack and Margaret and their own ancestors — information which I later incorporated in my first novel, "Farewell Forever." It began as just a family story for my children and grandchildren but eventually reached more than five hundred readers in the U.S. and Ireland.

I was almost a year old when my great-grandfather, Tom Malone, passed away in his ninetieth year on May 9, 1936. Although I have no real memory of him, I like to think that he might have held me on his lap when I was a baby. My father knew him well and used to tell me and my sisters the old stories about Grandpa Tom and his family. Now I have eight grandchildren of my own, my father is long gone, and I treasure every one of those old family stories.

Before my own time comes, I want to set down in an accessible form the story of Tom and Roxa Malone so that it will not simply be forgotten, as so many family stories are these days. Here, then, is my story of Tom and Roxa, partly fact, as far as the facts are still known, but mostly fiction in its details, filling in the many gaps that only they themselves could fill if they were still here with us. And, sometimes, as I spend lonely hours at the keyboard writing their story, I feel as if they *are* still here, reading over my shoulder and prompting me when I get things wrong.

Chapter One: 1862

The Malone children crowded together in the tiny kitchen where their parents were discussing the latest war news arriving on the stagecoaches traveling west on the National Road from nearby Cumberland, Maryland. Their father, Jack Malone, still in his early forties but already crippled and bent by painful rheumatism from his twenty years of hard work as a road mender, had just arrived home for his evening "tea" from his new job as toll keeper on the huge wooden covered bridge spanning the Monongahela River in south-western Pennsylvania. He was usually the first person in West Brownsville to hear any important news from the outside world.

"Jaysus, Mary and Joseph, Margaret. They say those starving rebs are after eating up all the poor farmers' livestock over there in Mary-land. Fifty thousand of 'em crossed the Potomac at White's Ferry last night."

Their mother, Margaret Malone, a dour, forty-year-old Ulsterwoman, worn out by bearing eight children and burying three of them, looked up from preparing their evening meal, wiped her hands on her apron, frowned at her husband and crossed herself. "Arragh, Jack. What's to become of us if they ever reach Pennsylvania?"

Pete, their eldest, nineteen and full of bravado, laughed scornfully. "Don't you worry none, Mam, we'll chase them thieving scoundrels right back to Virginny."

His younger brother, Tom, fifteen, piped up, "Who you talking about, Pete? I don't see you carrying no gun." For this Tom earned a hard punch on the arm that made him wince.

Jack raised his voice, "Stop them monkeyshines, ye two spalpeens. Shut up now and help yer Mam with the tay."

Tom stuck out his tongue and made a face at his brother, who pretended not to notice. Pete Malone was a handsome young man, proudly sporting a thin beard and a wispy moustache, with the same fair good looks – blond hair and bright blue eyes – that his mother had once possessed before frequent child-bearing had aged her so terribly. Pete's bold, dashing appearance made many a young girl's heart skip a beat when he attended Mass at Saint Peter's across the river on a Sunday morning.

Tom, on the other hand, was less striking in appearance, favoring his father's hirsute, "black Irish" looks. He'd been a blue-eyed towhead as an infant, but his hair had turned almost completely black by the time he entered puberty. He was short and powerfully built for a fifteen year-old, but slow and deliberate in his movements, unlike his brother, who was graceful and quick.

The brothers pretended to help their mother and sisters lay the table for the evening meal, banging and rattling the dishes on purpose. They knew their older sister Mary would step in and take over from their artful clumsiness. Stout, good-hearted Mary Malone was seventeen, plain in appearance and already resigned to helping her aging parents around the house. Alas, poor Mary made nobody's heart skip a beat at Sunday Mass.

The two younger sisters, Ellen, eight, and Katie, five, helped their mother serve their simple supper, boiled potatoes with ham hocks and cabbage. As usual, the family ate quickly and in complete silence, cleared the dishes and knelt together for the family Rosary. Days were getting shorter, and the Malones did not waste money on candles or lamps. They quickly prepared for sleep and went off to their straw-filled ticking mattresses, Tom and Pete sharing one up in the loft. As soon as Jack and Margaret started snoring behind their curtain, Pete nudged Tom, gently this time. "Tom, wake up. Can you keep a secret?"

"Sure I can. What is it?"

"They're forming a new cavalry company in Beallsville tomorrow, Pennsylvania volunteers to kick Johnny Reb back across the Potomac. I know Mam and Da would never agree. They think the Irish always get stuck with fighting other people's wars for them. But I'm going over there to enlist anyway. I'll be up and out o' here before sunup. Will you come with me?"

Tom's heart swelled at the realization that Pete, his idol, wanted him to enlist in the same regiment – to be his comrade in arms. Without thinking, he blurted, "Sure I'll come with you, Pete. We'll be the fighting Malone brothers, together through thick and thin, chasing the rebels back to Virginny."

"Put 'er there, little brother," whispered Pete, clasping Tom's hand in his.

The eastern sky was turning from rosy gray to peach behind them as the two brothers neared the top of Indian Hill, the western bluff above the Monongahela River. It was chilly, and their young bodies were grateful for the exercise warming them as they trudged up the steep graveled road from the still-sleeping town.

"They must be awake by now, Tom." said Pete, slightly out of breath from the long climb. "But it's Saturday morning, so they'll prob'ly think we just went over the bridge to Brownsville looking for some fun."

"Yeah, they'll never suspect that we're leaving home to enlist." replied Tom, struggling to keep up with the longer stride of his brother. "Heck, they prob'ly won't even miss us 'til this evening."

As they breasted the top of the hill, the first rays of the sun touched the bottoms of the scattered wisps of cloud in the sky behind them, turning them to streaks of bright orange light. Tom could see a few teams and wagons ahead in the distance, overlanders up early this September morning and already moving west with all their family and belongings packed in the big Conestoga "prairie schooners". The war had lessened the flow of migrants to the West but had not stopped it.

Tom felt proud and happy that Pete had asked him to come along with him to Beallsville, but he was also starting to feel scared and sad to be leaving home for the first time and going off to war. Still, Pennsylvania – his state – had been invaded by the Rebs, and, by golly, he wasn't going to sit at home with his sisters and the old folks while men were fighting and dying and Pete was risking his life to defend them.

Beallsville was normally just a wide place in the road with a few taverns, a market and a drovers' yard, but it was crowded that morning with people from all over Washington County. A small, improvised band was struggling with patriotic march tunes, peppered with occasional sour and off-beat notes. Some of the men were accompanied by wives, sweethearts and children, come to see their men folk off to war. The carnival atmosphere in the market square was dampened by their tears as fond farewells were being said, perhaps for the last time.

Pete and Tom stood in a long line of men, slowly snaking its way toward a table manned by a lieutenant and two sergeants, who were taking particulars and writing in the muster rolls. A doctor was on hand to examine any recruits thought to be questionable on medical grounds.

Pete was accepted without hesitation as a private in Company D of the 22nd Pennsylvania Cavalry. Then it was Tom's turn. Tom had been taught always to tell the truth, and, when the lieutenant asked, "How old are you, sonny?" he replied, "I'm almost sixteen, sir, only three weeks short of it."

The lieutenant conferred with the sergeants and then turned back to Tom. "I'm afraid you're still too young, Tom. And besides, we don't like to take two brothers away from their parents. You're a brave lad, though, and I thank you for coming here today." He smiled and extended his hand to Tom. It was over.

Tom's heart sank, and he couldn't stop the tears that blurred his eyes as he searched for Pete in the crowd. Finally he saw him standing under a tree, talking to a couple of pretty young girls. Rushing toward them, he blurted, "They wouldn't take me, Pete.

Said I was too young. And they don't want to take two brothers away from their folks."

"Sorry, Tom. It would've been grand, us chasing the rebs together, the fighting Malone brothers. You'd best be on your way back home now, though, if you want to be there before dark. Tell Mam and Da goodbye for me."

Tom wanted to grab Pete and hug him. What if he would never see his big brother again? He knew other folks in the Three Towns who had already lost loved ones in the year since the war had started. He wiped the tears from his eyes, embarrassed by the stares of the two girls. "So long, Pete. Take care of yourself," he murmured. Then, with a heavy heart, he walked slowly away, headed east on the National Road.

The hickory stick whistled through the air and landed with a crack on Tom's bare back, sending a wave of agony through him. "What the divil were ye thinking, ye poor *amadan*, ye. Letting yer brother run off like that without telling us."

Tom clenched his teeth against the sharp pain, determined not to cry out, as his father gave him twenty hard strokes with the slim hickory rod. He was no longer a boy, whether the army thought so or not. He was a man now, and, whether he deserved it or not, he would take his punishment like a man.

Chapter Two: 1864

Although the Malone house was still shrouded in shadows, Tom could see sunlight filtering through the dirt and cobwebs in the small window pane opposite his solitary bed in the loft. The first rays of the sun peeped over the hilltops across the river to the east, above the little log cabin where he had first seen its light just eighteen years earlier, silhouetting the bronze cross atop the steeple of the stone church his father had helped to build the year before he was born.

His parents must have been happier in those days. His Da had not yet been crippled by rheumatism from the heavy road work, and his Mam had not been worn out from delivering the eight babies and then having to bury three of the little ones in the churchyard now flooding with sunshine across the river. He wished he had known them then. Now, with their darling Pete gone off to war in Virginia two years before, evenings at home were mostly somber affairs of silent meals and long sighs. All the life seemed to have gone out of the two of them.

As with most other things, Pete was careless about writing letters home, and Jack and Margaret Malone were struggling to learn how to read from the girls so that they could decipher the few precious letters themselves and not have to sit and listen as one of their children read them aloud.

After they gave him that thrashing, their anger had apparently been quenched, and they no longer seemed to harbor any hard feelings about Pete's running off to join the cavalry. The incident had left Tom full of resentment and anger, longing to get away from home like his brother and make his own way in the world. Now that he was finally eighteen, he was determined to leave them. Today, by God, he would do it.

Bill Walsh, the foreman down at the boatyard where Tom worked, told him a month ago that the biggest local coal mine operator, Captain William H. Brown of Pittsburgh, was hiring more hands to man his growing fleet of towboats. Lincoln's military draft in '63 had taken too many men away from work on the river, poor men who could not afford the three-hundred-dollar rich man's exemption or who hired themselves as substitutes for the drafted rich men. And now, with October only a few days away, "coalboat water" had arrived on the Monongahela, and navigation down the river from the mines was already beginning, advanced several months by early fall rains in the Alleghenies.

Tom read every bit of news about the war that he could lay his hands on. General Sherman's Army of the Tennessee had finally taken Atlanta four weeks earlier, forcing all the citizens to evacuate and then, as punishment for their stubborn resistance, burning almost the entire city to the ground. Now, Sherman's sixty-two thousand tough veterans were waiting in Atlanta to begin their final march to the sea.

During the dry summer months of low water, hundreds of thousands of tons of coal and supplies had piled up in Quartermaster's depots along the upper Ohio and Mississippi Rivers. The army and the navy needed those supplies as they fought their way farther into the heart of the South, driving iron-clad wedges down the Mississippi and into Georgia, right through the heart of the divided Confederate forces.

Since Pete had gone off two years earlier to what was now called "West Virginia" to search for Confederate raiders in the hills around Moorefield, Lost River and Petersburg with his Beallsville Cavalry comrades, Tom had worked at odd jobs in the busy boatyard in West Brownsville. All the boatyards in the

Ohio Valley were turning out new steam-powered towboats as fast as they could to meet the growing demands of the Quartermaster's Department.

Tom would have preferred to sign on as a deckhand on one of the new towboats long ago, but he was still under eighteen then, too young to be a crew member, and so he did his best at the available jobs around the boatyard, getting to know the boat owners and captains in the process and deciding that he would much rather stay close to the river than go off on horseback to the hills of West Virginia like Pete. He did not like horses at all.

He dressed carefully and trimmed his new beard and moustache, brushing the wispy dark hairs to make them look thicker. He would go first to St. Peter's Parochial House to obtain from Father Heaney, the new Pastor, a certificate of baptism that would show his date of birth, September 29, 1846.

"How are ye, Tom?" Bill Walsh, the burly Irish foreman, smoke from his smelly old pipe curling around his head, stood at the entrance to the boatyard as Tom walked by. "Are ye not coming to work in the yard today?"

"Not today, Bill. Today I'm looking fer a deckhand's berth on the Brown's Line. It's my birthday today, and I'm eighteen years old."

"That right? Well, ye're in luck, then, bucko. Brown's are up here hiring some crew for the *Shark* out of Pittsburgh this very moment. Captain Sam hisself came up t'day with one of the pool boats, picking up a tow o' coal from the Alicia Mine fer the *Shark* to take to the Quartermaster's down in Memphis. The *Shark's* too big to work up here on the Mon. She just tows coal out o' Brown's Yard down in Pittsburgh, but this time the Captain's got hisself a *charter*, so he has. Gets paid by the gov'ment every day, even while the *Shark's* laid up down there waiting fer the tow to build. Sure beats charging by the bushel, don't it?"

"That it does, Bill, that it does. Tell me, is Captain Sam looking for deckhands, d'ye know?"

Tom's heart quickened. He remembered the *Shark*, a hundred sixty eight feet long, with a thirty-three foot beam width, a five foot draft and almost five hundred tons burden, launched just two years earlier from this very same boatyard. She was powerful and fast, too big for the Mon River. Like most towboats of her class, she normally carried a complement of eighteen officers and crew, including four deckhands, two for each six-hour watch.

"He's a couple o' deckhands short, Tom. One o' the young spalpeens got drunk t'other night in Pittsburgh and fell in the river and drownded. Another fella had a bad accident while they was building the tow at Brown's Station. He'll be laid up fer a while. Sure, the strong drink is the Irishman's curse." Tom knew that at least half of the deckhands on the river were Irish immigrants. Only a few were native-born Americans like himself.

"Thanks, Bill." Tom waved and started toward the bridge. "I'd better get right on over to the wharf and see Captain Sam 'fore he up and hires somebody else."

As he arrived at Water Street, just above the wharf, Tom could see all the cabin windows on the starboard side of the pool boat's boiler deck. Captain Samuel S. Brown, son of the owner, was sitting in the dining room adjacent to his cabin, drinking coffee from a heavy china mug as the cook cleared away the remains of his breakfast.

Tom hailed him through the open windows, asking for permission to come aboard. "Captain Sam" was only twenty-two, just a year older than Pete, but he had already survived the Mississippi River naval battles of Memphis and Vicksburg, and, once again a civilian, now had his father's fleet to command.

"C'mon down here, Tom. I figured you might be showing up one of these days. So you heard about my deckhands, did you?" Captain Sam knew Tom as the eager kid working at the West Brownsville boatyard. The Brown's Line towboats occasionally laid up there for repairs and maintenance during the summer months, when navigation on the upper rivers ceased.

"Today's my birthday, Captain. I'm old enough to sign on. Will you hire me, sir? I've been working around boats fer the last two years, and I know most everything I need to know to be a deckhand."

"We're hurting for crew, Tom, I'll tell you honest. New boats are being launched every day, and the government contracts keep rolling in. We now have to pay fifty dollars a month for young Irish deckhands, thanks to Abe Lincoln's draft."

Tom shook his head in awe at the figure. The going wage had doubled since the first year of the war. "I hear you got the *Shark* chartered, Captain. That right?"

"You bet, Tom. If I wasn't operating on a charter, I wouldn't be setting here having a second cup of coffee and wasting valuable time. I'd be out there looking for more business." He reached across the table for a file folder with the paper for himself and Tom to sign. "Here you are, Tom, fifty dollars a month, fully found. Employment month to month with no guarantees on either side. Just sign right there."

Tom signed the paper eagerly, his hand trembling so with excitement that he blotted the ink. At last he was free. No more putting up with his kid sisters' childish prattle and the continual complaints of the "old folks". He, too, was finally going off to help the Union fight the war by delivering coal to the navy.

"Get yourself over to the mine tipple now, Tom, and help the others round up the loaded coalboats and build the tow. The day's just started, and we're already running late, so look lively."

Jack Malone was still on duty at the tollhouse on the huge wooden covered bridge when Tom crossed the river on his way back home that evening. "Where've ye bin, son? I thought ye was working at the yard today."

"Naw, Da, I got me new job. I signed on as a deckhand on the *Shark* today. We're taking a tow from Pittsburgh down to the Quartermaster's in Tennessee. Just want to go home and pack my things. I'll be sleeping on board tonight cuz we're picking up the tow in the morning."

Jack shrugged. "Yer Mam'll not be happy ye're leaving, boy. She and Mary are after cooking ye a good supper fer yer birt'day.

Get on home now and tell 'em I'll come as soon as me relief shows up."

So that was all, thought Tom. His life had changed completely, and the old man just sat there, puffing on his damned pipe, talking about supper. No "happy birthday", nothing. He felt a stitch in his heart for an instant, remembering the pain of the old man's beating two years earlier. He swallowed the lump in his throat, turned away, and marched home, his face burning and angry tears clouding his eyes. They still thought of him as a child.

Tom heard his mother busy in her kitchen, surrounded like a mother hen by her three daughters, who shuttled to and from the table with dishes of food. As he came in the front door, there was a flurry of footsteps and whispers. "Quick now, girls, get that cake out of sight. Yer brother's coming."

Tom hesitated a moment before entering the kitchen, listening to the scuffle within as the girls tried to hide his "surprise" birthday cake. "I'm home." he called out. He could see the dishes assembled on the table. They contained all his favorite foods: a whole roasted, stuffed chicken, mashed potatoes, giblet gravy, peas and Indian pudding for dessert. The delicious aromas mingled in his nostrils, making his mouth water.

"I've got wonderful news. I just got a job as deckhand on the *Shark*, with Captain Sam Brown himself. We're leaving in the morning from Pittsburgh with a tow of Alicia coal for the U.S. Navy. Got to keep our gunboats steaming, now that we control the rivers again. I'll be sleeping on board tonight, 'cuz we're leaving the first thing in the morning."

A chilly silence descended on the kitchen, and Margaret Malone banged down the cooking spoon she was using to stir the gravy. "Ye're the great one fer surprises, aren't ye, Tom?" she snarled, "The last time ye did this to us, it got ye a thrashing. Don't ye be expecting us to be happy fer ye. 'Tis bad enough that yer brother ran off to the war without a word. You boys will break yer poor mother's heart yet, so ye will." She broke into tears, hiding her face with her apron.

Once again, Tom felt the old hurt rising in his throat, "I've got to go pack my bag now, Mam," he mumbled, "Da said to tell you he'll be home as soon as his relief shows up." He wanted to shout at her. He wanted to break something. He wondered why he even bothered to tell anyone his news as he climbed up to the loft to pack his things. He'd be damned if he would eat any of her birthday supper, cake or no cake.

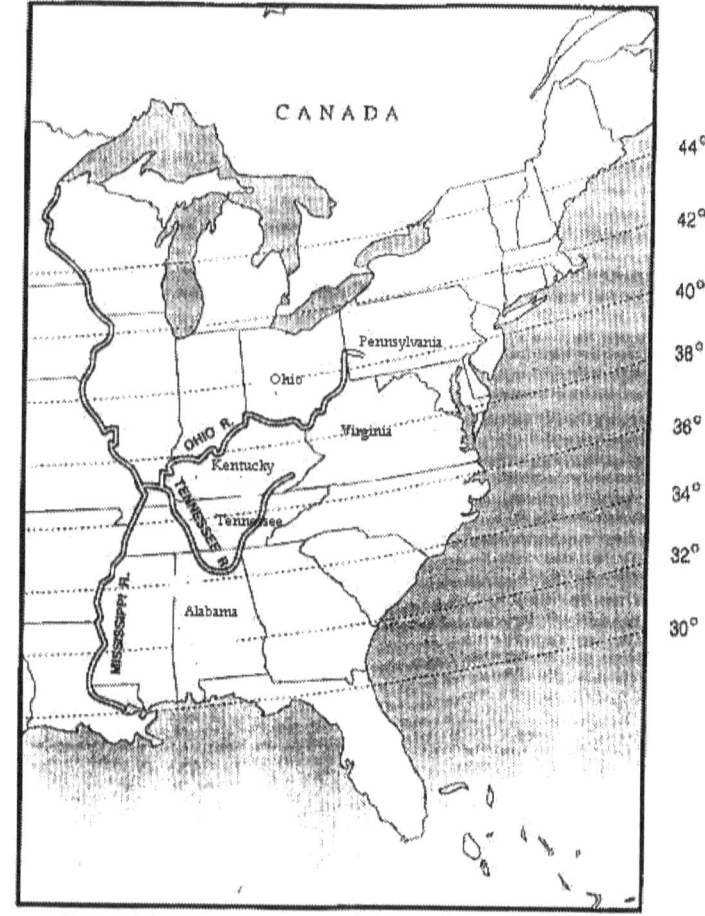

Pre-war Map of the Mississippi, Ohio and Tennessee Rivers

Chapter Three:

The Ohio River had reached its lowest stage – only three feet of water at Cincinnati – on August 6 that year. Then the river began to rise again, much earlier than usual. By the end of September navigation had already fully resumed. Hundreds of towboats, barges and transports, many of them brand new, had headed downstream, carrying the summer's backlog of supplies and troop reinforcements southward, borne over the rocks, bars and shoals by the rapidly rising waters and protected by a large fleet of Union gunboats.

The *Shark* had already delivered her first two tows of coal to U.S. Navy coaling stations at Cairo and Memphis on the Mississippi, and, toward the end of October, she was back again in Pittsburgh, picking up another tow. This time the coal was destined for the new Federal supply depot called "Johnsonville," seventy-eight miles west of Nashville at a railhead on the Tennessee River.

Tom had just received his very first deckhand's pay, fifty greenback dollars, and was walking home across the big bridge from the Alicia Mine to visit his family before the pool boat departed again for Pittsburgh the next day. He had mostly gotten over his hurt feelings about the disastrous birthday supper and was embarrassed as he remembered his ungrateful behavior that evening. He had acted like a child. No wonder they didn't take him seriously. He would apologize to all of them, do the manly thing, and give his mother part of the money he had earned. The rest would go for some warm clothes for the approaching winter.

His father had already gone from the tollhouse on the bridge as Tom crossed the six hundred foot span to West Brownsville. The family would be surprised to see him, he thought. He had brought a few inexpensive souvenirs from Memphis for the girls, and his parents would be happy to receive some of his pay. Maybe he would spend the night with them, sleeping up in the loft the way he used to.

His mouth was dry and his heart quickened as he approached the little house. His face burned with shame. He could hear voices from the kitchen as he walked in the door. "Hello. It's me, Tom" he called and then awkwardly blurted out, "and I'm so sorry fer the way I acted when I left on my birthday. I'm really sorry. I didn't mean to hurt your feelings so, you and the girls. Look, Mam, I got my pay today. And this is for you."

He reached out his hand with twenty dollars in it, a huge sum for the Malone family. Margaret Malone's usual dour expression softened a little, and she even managed a fleeting smile as she took the money. "We'll say no more about your birthday, Tommy. You missed a fine chicken supper, cake and all, and the more fool you." Not a word of thanks for his hard-earned dollars as she tucked them away in her pocket.

Tom shrugged and turned away, climbing the ladder to the loft to unpack his bag. He found the souvenirs he had bought for his sisters and brought them back down to the kitchen. "Where's Da?" he asked, "He already left the bridge before I got there."

The three girls looked to their mother for a reply. She frowned and shook her head. "Your Da's likely stopping off at the tavern again on his way home. He tells us he needs a hot whiskey after work to ease his rheumatism in this damp weather we've been having. I wouldn't mind if he only took the one, but since you left fer the river, he's been rolling home at any old hour, singing Fenian ballads and late fer his supper."

"But, Mam, didn't ye tell us Da took the pledge back in Ireland? When did he start drinking whiskey again?"

"He was fine as long as he could do the hard work on the road, but when his rheumatism got too much for him, he started drinking. Just a little at first, but this past month that ye've been away on the river, sure 'tis every day now, and I can tell ye, Tom, this money ye gave me comes in handy, what with him drinking up half his pay." She sighed and shook her head again, wiping a tear from the corner of her eye with the back of her hand.

Without thinking, Tom reached out to his mother and tried to take her in his arms to comfort her. She turned away from him, shoving him back with one hand. "Go along wit' ye, now. Leave me be. Supper's ready, and we'll eat it while it's hot. We'll not be waiting fer the ould fella to come home."

After the usual silent supper and the nightly family Rosary, Tom helped his sisters with the dishes before settling down to recount his experiences of his trips down the Ohio and Mississippi to Memphis.

Mary, at nineteen already well on her way to spinsterhood and apprenticed to a local seamstress, quizzed him eagerly about the ladies' fashions he had observed during his visits ashore. "And the hats, Tom? What kind of hats were they wearing?"

"I dunno, Mary. They looked like plain ol' bonnets to me." She rolled her eyes heavenward in exasperation as Tom shrugged and scratched his head, trying to remember something, anything, that might interest her.

Ellen, ten, and Katie, seven, were content to play with the trinkets he had brought for them as, dishes washed and put away, the family gathered by the fire to await the belated return of Jack Malone from the neighborhood tavern. Finally, he arrived, flushed and sweating from a series of hot whiskeys in spite of the raw, damp cold. Unusually jolly and reeking of cheap whiskey, he gave Tom a bear hug and kissed him on the cheek. "Ach, Tom, 'tis glad I am to see ye. How are ye, son?"

"I'm fine, Da. How are you?" Was this the same man he had angrily walked out on a month ago, Tom wondered?

Then Jack Malone recalled his rheumatism and all his other woes, and his demeanor suddenly changed to that of a long-suffering, self-pitying invalid. "Ah, well, Tom. This nasty weather's got me down, don't ye know?" he whimpered. It was as if he had just aged ten years before Tom's eyes. Gone was the jolly, drunken stranger, and there in his place was his Da, the familiar defeated figure, looking older and sadder than his forty-five years could possibly warrant.

At that moment, Tom filled with pity for his father, in spite of the accumulated hurts he had received from him over the years. There he stood, Jack Malone, once a proud man among men in the local community, now deserted by his sons and left to seek sympathy and male companionship at the local tavern.

Tom thought of his young crewmates on the *Shark,* the hard work and good times they shared and the bonds of manly friendship they were already forging in his first month as a deckhand. His Da had to sit alone all day in the tollhouse on the bridge, waiting for another person to talk to. No wonder he stopped at the tavern before going home to his girls and their mother. He reached out his hand and patted his father on the shoulder. Though part of him still feared his father, Tom thought he really did love the "ould fella" in spite of their past differences. He felt a pang of guilt, remembering that he had to be back aboard the pool boat at daybreak. His new freedom came with a price. Would he always feel guilty every time he left home to return to the river? Was the river in fact becoming his real home, the rivermen his real family?

After traveling more than nine hundred miles down the Ohio River from Pittsburgh to Paducah in only two days and nights, the *Shark's* pilot carefully maneuvered her into the narrow channel of the Tennessee River, making a hairpin turn to the left against the powerful combined currents of the two rivers while avoiding the many shoals, bars and snags at their confluence. Then, at dawn on the morning of Friday, October 28, they began the hundred mile upstream trip to Johnsonville, pushing the tow against the powerful flood.

As they started upstream, they passed another steamboat heading down toward Paducah. The captain of the other boat shouted to them through his megaphone, "Be careful, there's Confederate raiders up in Tennessee trying to stop us from delivering supplies and reinforcements." Before Captain Sam could get any details, the two steamboats had already passed each other and his shouted reply was lost in the whoosh of the 'scape pipes and the swish of the two great paddlewheels churning the muddy floodwaters at their sterns.

Just before noon, they were sixty miles above Paducah approaching Fort Henry and Fort Heiman, abandoned Confederate forts that glowered at each other on opposite sides of the river like two toothless dragons. Tom was out on the front of the tow watching for snags. Suddenly he heard an unfamiliar sound in the distance. At first he thought it was thunder, but then he realized he was hearing cannon fire and the crackle of muskets, sounds he had only heard during Fourth of July celebrations back home in Brownsville.

He knew Captain Sam and the others would not be able to hear the sound of the shooting back in wheelhouse, where it would be drowned out by the noise of the engines, 'scape pipes and paddlewheel. He ran along the gunwales back to the boat to warn them. "Captain, sounds like we're heading into a fight up ahead. I think I heard guns firing."

Captain Sam thought a minute, then spoke to the pilot, "Find a place to stop her and tie up out of the current. I'll take a couple of the deckhands in the yawl boat and row upstream to have a look-see. No need to risk the towboat and the cargo." In the small yawl boat, Tom realized, they could stay in the shallow water out of the main channel and make better headway against the current. Also, they might be able observe the battle without being noticed or walk the bank hidden in the underbrush.

"I'll need two strong volunteers to row the yawl boat. You're one of them, Malone. Kelly, you're the other." Seamus Kelly, Tom's bunkmate on the *Shark*, nodded and touched his cap. He was a huge, hairy young man with a red beard and a complexion to match, recently come over from Ireland. He had somehow managed to avoid being conscripted into the army on his arrival on the dock in Philadelphia. He spoke English with a thick Irish brogue, but, having worked his passage across the Atlantic, he had a good knowledge of boats and had taken quickly to the duties of a deckhand.

As the *Shark's* engines slowed to a stop in the quiet shallows at the mouth of Yellow Spring Branch, the two deckhands scrambled ashore to make her fast to large trees. With the river in flood, many trees stood easily within reach in the water along the banks. The *Shark* could safely remain there in the trees inside the river bend, hidden from view both upstream and downstream, while the captain and his two "volunteers" went on ahead to see what was happening. The yawl boat, a sturdy but graceful sixteen-foot skiff propelled by four oars, was quickly launched, and the three men jumped aboard and set forth up the swollen river toward the steady sound of artillery, muskets and small arms fire.

They had only rowed a couple of miles when the firing suddenly ceased. Captain Sam took out his gold pocket watch and checked the time. "An hour and a half of firing." he muttered, "That must have been some fight."

Then they saw a terrifying sight. Just rounding the next bend was a big steam packet, riddled with shot holes, her port smokestack blown off. She was moving slowly downstream toward them.

"It's the *Anna*, boys." said Captain Sam. "She usually runs between Cincinnatti and Pittsburgh. I know Captain Maratta and his son Bill. Looks like her steam line's damaged. Let's hail her and see if we can go aboard."

They rowed out into the channel while the *Anna* drifted downstream with the current, her paddlewheel barely turning and steam escaping from the damaged line. Captain J.H. Maratta, badly shaken, welcomed them aboard.

"Hello, Sam. What the hell're you boys doing out here?"

"We heard a lot of shooting, Cap'n. Looks like you were on the receiving end."

"That's for sure, Sam. There was a whole swarm of Forrest's cavalry waiting for us with ten o' them twelve-pounder Napoleon field guns at Paris Landing this morning. If they hadn't nicked my steam line with a lucky shot back there, we'd be long gone fer Paducah by now. Without any power to the engines, though, we just had to sit there and take it 'til we floated out of their range."

"Anybody get hurt, Cap'n?"

"Yeah, one of their sharpshooters nicked my son Bill in the shoulder but missed the bone, thank God. And Jim Mortimer, our pilot, got a bullet right through his hat, and another one hit the wheel and knocked a splinter into his hand."

He took his four visitors up to the hurricane deck, where they counted thirty bullet holes and a cannon shot through the pilot house bulkheads. Captain Sam shook his head and let out a long whistle. Although he was still sweating from the exertion of rowing the yawl boat, Tom suddenly began to shiver. It was unbelievable that no one had died in that deadly rain of hot metal.

The *Anna* finally drifted abreast of the *Shark,* still tethered to trees around the bend in the river. Captain Sam and the boys said goodbye to the lucky survivors aboard the crippled *Anna* and returned to their own boat. "What'll we do now, Captain?" asked Tom.

"I guess we'll wait here 'til nightfall and then see if we can't sneak past their guns in the dark by staying way over on the Tennessee side of the river."

That night they were in luck. As the *Shark* approached the two abandoned forts, all her lights extinguished, a sudden cloudburst drenched them as thunder rumbled, drowning out the noise of the engine, 'scape pipes and paddlewheel. Through the downpour they saw soldiers busily moving their artillery into firing positions in the abandoned upper batteries of Fort Heiman on the high bluff above them. Although the soldiers were concentrating on their work and not paying attention to the river, Captain Sam slowed the *Shark's* engines to a crawl to minimize the noise and steered close to the far side of the river, where the flood still provided just enough water for their loaded coalboats to pass. After a few endless, terrifying minutes they passed the fort unnoticed by the Confederate bivouac.

"Okay, boys, you can breathe again," laughed Captain Sam, "The rebs must have come down here from Paris Landing after they hit the *Anna*. No telling where they're headed next, but since they're moving north, we'd best keep moving south. Uncle Sam's navy needs this coal."

After steaming for another thirty-eight miles, they finally reached the new Federal depot called "Johnsonville." Hundreds of colored soldiers were working methodically in the pouring rain, unloading the last of the supplies for Sherman's Army from the fleet of transports and barges moored to the long row of wharfboats along the water's edge. Other colored troops were standing guard duty or manning the battery of field guns lined up on the bank between the rail sidings and the wharfboats. Groups of white soldiers, many missing arms or legs or wearing bandages, sheltered under the overhanging eaves of the warehouses, waiting to be taken back downriver away from the war. A long row of closed pine coffins waited with them.

After delivering his cargo manifest to the Harbor Master, Captain Sam walked up to the HQ, a small building beside the rail depot, and informed Colonel Thompson, the commander of the garrison, that the Confederates had occupied Fort Heiman during the night and had positioned their field artillery behind the earthworks on top of the bluff. Colonel Thompson frowned and shook his head, concerned by the unexpected news.

"There are no less than six navy gunboats here," he growled, "and they and two transports, the *Venus* and the *Cheesman*, have been waiting here several days for the coal you brought. I'm afraid we'll just have to send the transports downriver with a navy escort once their bunkers are full. It may be risky, but we can't wait any longer. In the meantime I've received a telegram from the Quartermaster's that a load of your coal is urgently needed farther upriver. You and the *Shark* are to proceed immediately to Decatur, Alabama, and deliver that coal to the navy."

Captain Sam whistled. "Decatur's above the Muscle Shoals rapids, Colonel. What's going on up there? Can you tell us?"

"Don't know all the details, Captain, but it seems that Hood's entire Army of Tennessee escaped from Sherman's trap and came north from Atlanta to Decatur. Meanwhile Sherman had taken his sixty thousand men back to Atlanta by a different route, leaving Thomas with a small force to defend Tennessee. Just like two ships passing in the night." Sam shook his head and frowned.

"Then, just three days ago, the rebels unexpectedly arrived in front of Decatur," Colonel Thompson went on, "and our outnumbered troops in the fort were surrounded and besieged. To top it all off, we learned just this morning that the main force of Hood's army has already left Decatur again and is moving off to the west along the south bank of the river, probably looking for an easier place to cross. Even though badly outnumbered, Decatur was too tough a nut for the secesh to crack. The *General Sherman* and the other navy "tinclads" on the Upper Tennessee have been helping the army to defend it and keep the rebels from crossing there, but their coal is running low, so we need to send you up there just as fast as we can."

"How come you can't send the coal to Decatur on the railroad, Colonel? The *Shark's* one of the best towboats on the river, but, even with this high water, I'm not sure I can get her up the Muscle Shoals rapids against the flood current, let alone pushing a loaded coalboat."

"Normally, we would send the navy's coal up to Nashville from here and then on down the railroad to Decatur, but a few weeks ago Forrest's cavalry crossed the river into Alabama at Waterloo, destroyed the railroad between Alabama and Tennessee, and then escaped back across the river to Mississippi. They even burned down the Sulphur Branch Trestle and captured our little fort there. Took all the survivors back down south with them as prisoners. I'm afraid it'll be quite a while before we can ship anything to Decatur by rail, Captain."

Later, as he listened to Captain Sam relating the colonel's news to the crew, Tom marveled at the audacity and swiftness of

Forrest's Confederate cavalry, coming all the way back to the Kentucky border and blockading the river less than three weeks after high tailing off to Mississippi following a successful raid on the Alabama-Tennessee rail line.

His heart sank as he thought of the ordeal that awaited them a hundred forty miles farther up the river. Not only must they ascend the treacherous Muscle Shoals rapids but they also must run the gauntlet between the two armies poised for battle on opposite banks of the Tennessee River.

Chapter Four

They arrived in Alabama as planned, before daybreak on Sunday morning, October 30. The pilot needed as many hours of daylight as possible to follow the narrow, twisting channel up through the three main rapids, climbing over a hundred feet vertically in less than thirty miles.

Heavy rain was falling, adding to the already swollen river. The *Shark* began to encounter stronger currents and turbulence a few miles upstream from Waterloo, the town where Forrest's cavalry had crossed and re-crossed the river a few weeks earlier when he had wreaked havoc on the Nashville-Decatur Railroad.

After their close call with Forrest's men back in Kentucky and then hearing that Hood's entire force of thirty thousand was heading toward them from Decatur, the crew of the *Shark* was posted on high alert, expecting to be fired on at any moment by the Confederate pickets plainly visible along the south bank of the swollen river. They were hardly reassured by the sparseness of the Union pickets patrolling the north bank.

Tom and his bunkmate, Seamus Kelly, were stationed forward on the head of the coalboat, holding long barge poles and nervously watching for boulders and snags in the swirling water. Although the river was very high, they could see ripples and swells on the surface where rocky ledges and large boulders lay submerged under the muddy water. The *Shark's* progress had slowed to a crawl, partly due to the need for caution, but also because the speed of the current was increasing as they entered the first of the three rapids, Colbert's Shoals.

"Captain Sam's not at all happy with this trip, Seamus. Says he don't want to lose the *Shark* on account of one load of coal, orders or no orders."

"Ach, Tom, now don't ye worry none. Sure, we've a fine pilot at the wheel, now haven't we, and aren't we picking our way through the rocks and shoals like we're walking on egg shells? Captain Sam'll pull us through, right enough. You'll see."

The rest of their watch was spent at the front of the coalboat, frantically fending off from the rocks and snags as best they could while maintaining their balance on the slippery, rain-wet narrow deck. At the end of their six hours, they gratefully handed their poles to the other two deckhands and scrambled back to the *Shark* for some dry clothes and coffee, followed by a hot meal and deep, exhausted sleep.

Late in the afternoon they finally reached Decatur, formerly the main railroad junction on the Tennessee River and the scene of a three day siege that had ended only the day before their arrival. After dropping the coalboat off at the navy coaling station, the captain and crew went ashore to visit the Union fort that, with its back to the river, encircled the ruins of the town. The fort had been constructed during the summer using lumber scavenged by the careful dismantling of every wooden building in Decatur following the withdrawal of the Confederate forces to defend Atlanta earlier in the year. Only three isolated masonry buildings remained standing. The civilian population had all been forced to evacuate, and their freed slaves had been hired by the army to build the new wooden fort.

Seamus had been in Decatur before and offered to show Tom around. "Let's walk up to the rail junction, boyo. I want to show ye something ye'll never forget." From the piers of the burned-out bridge at the river's edge, they walked south along the railway right of way until they reached what had once been the main line of the Memphis and Charleston Railroad, connecting northern Alabama with the Mississippi. Near the charred ruin of the engine house they saw piles of iron rails stretching off in the distance to the west. Union troops had torn up the rails when they had destroyed the vital Confederate supply link. They had heated the rails red hot over burning piles of wooden sleepers until they were soft and pliable. They had then bent and twisted the hot rails to make them unusable, many of them formed into the letters U and S, called "Sherman's hairpins" by the Union troops.

Tom laughed and shook his head. "You're right, Seamus, I'll never forget seeing this. I'll probably be telling my grandchildren about it someday."

When they returned to the coaling station by the river, they found the USS *General Sherman*, a spanking new 187-ton side-wheel "tinclad" gunboat, already taking on coal from the load that the *Shark* had just delivered. The *General Sherman's* grateful commanding officer had invited the *Shark's* entire crew to inspect his gunboat and have Sunday supper as his guests in the navy mess before returning downriver. Their host explained that the gunboat, officially designated "Tinclad # 60," had been built in Chattanooga, turned over to the navy and commissioned in July. She had spent all of her three months' service on the Upper Tennessee in support of U.S. Army forces and had been instrumental in preventing Hood's army from crossing the river at Decatur the week before.

While they were all finishing their supper that evening a telegraph message arrived from General Hatch's Union forces in Florence, a large river town on the north shore just below the rapids. Hood had arrived with the vanguard of his army in Tuscumbia, across the river on the south side. He had brought his pontoons down from Decatur to Bainbridge, the last town on the upstream side of the rapids and was trying to rig a pontoon bridge there for his army to cross. The commanding officer of the *General Sherman* excused himself and rose from the table, barking orders to his officers to ready the gunboat for battle. Turning to Captain Sam, he warned, "You might want to follow us downstream, Sam. If the rebs make it across the river, your boat might be blockaded up here for God knows how long."

Captain Sam needed no urging. He too jumped up from the table and called his crew into action, ordering them to fire the boilers quickly and get up a head of steam. Much to their chagrin and embarrassment, Tom and Seamus were handed coal shovels and wheelbarrows too and ordered to help the colored firemen stoke the furnaces to speed up their departure. They would have to leave their coalboat behind in Decatur since it was still half full of coal, and they could not afford to wait for it to be emptied. Having no experience as firemen, Tom and Seamus fell to trundling wheelbarrows full of coal for the stokers.

Following closely in the wake of the gunboat, the *Shark* floated down the swollen river in the dark. Bainbridge was only forty miles below Decatur, but they wanted to approach it cautiously and arrive just before dawn if they could. Besides, if they could get past the rebel pontoon bridge, they would need daylight to descend the rapids beyond it. The *Shark* was like a giant baby chick following a miniature mother hen with less than half her tonnage. But she was unarmed and needed the protection of the eight big guns mounted on the *General Sherman*, a whole battery of floating artillery, surrounded by thick armor plate.

Tom and Seamus had the early watch, getting up and breakfasting before dawn. They put on their foul weather slickers and went out on the rain-washed deck to relieve the other watch. The *Shark's* engines were turning very slowly, just enough to maintain steerage way, as the swift current pushed the two boats along toward Bainbridge. The gunboat crew was already standing at their battle stations with all the gun ports open and the big cannons run out in firing position.

As the two boats reached Muscle Shoals, the shallow water above the first big rapids, the gray morning light began to reveal the shapes of trees along the low river banks, many of them flooded by the high water. Farther inland behind the trees on the south side of the river they could just make out some of the camp fires of Hood's Army of Tennessee, making their first cups of coffee. Confederate bivouacs were spread out for miles on the plain between the river and the Courtland road farther inland.

"Saints preserve us." gasped Seamus, crossing himself. "Would ye just look at that now, Tom? We must be passing by the whole Confederate Army."

Tom crossed himself too, awestruck by the evident numbers of the enemy, waiting to cross the flooded river and strike northward into Tennessee. He began to pray silently, his lips forming the familiar words, "Holy Mary, Mother of God, pray for us sinners now and at the hour of our death."

Ahead of them they could see the Confederate engineers in the distance still trying to rig their pontoon bridge. They had chosen Bainbridge as a narrow point in the river with banks still above the flood waters. But this meant that they had to contend with a much stronger current. Just downstream were the main rapids and no more feasible crossing points until the bridges of Union-occupied Florence.

Tom could hear volleys of small arms fire and the occasional bark of a twelve pound field howitzer from the northern bridgehead, which was under attack by Federal forces from the Florence garrison. When the southerners defending the nearly completed bridge saw the two steamboats coming toward them, they scrambled back over the bridge to safety, enabling the Union soldiers on shore to cut the north end of the bridge loose with axes. As the pontoons swung free, broadside to the strong current, several of them were swamped and capsized. The powerful force of the flood soon swept the loose end downstream into the rapids, damaging the bridge severely.

A loud cheer went up from the men on the gunboat and their companions on the *Shark*. As the gunboat swung around and headed back upstream to Decatur, its mission accomplished without firing a shot, Captain Sam blew a long blast on the *Shark's* whistle, thanking the navy for the escort. He then turned to the pilot and said, "Let's get back downriver quick before anything else happens."

Descending the rapids was a lot easier and faster than their long struggle upstream had been the day before. And, best of all, they had managed to slip past the whole Confederate Army of Tennessee and now had an easy ten-hour run back to the Federal depot at Johnsonville. There they would pick up their empties and return home to their base in Pittsburgh.

As the *Shark* rounded a bend in the river, the crew suddenly found themselves dangerously close to the Confederate pickets on the southern bank. One of the pickets, a tall, lanky man with a long beard and a battered, brown slouch hat, had a shooting rest and a short telescope sight on the left side of his Whitworth sharpshooter's rifle. He stood relaxed, his weight on one foot and his other knee slightly bent.

He could have passed for a farm boy, lounging on the front porch of a small town general store on a Saturday afternoon, were it not for the big rifle beside him. He was sheltered from the rain under a spreading live oak tree, watching them, taking his time to pick the right target. He finally raised his rifle and tucked it tight against his right cheek as he found his chosen victim in the cross-hairs of the scope. Someone on deck screamed "Look out." in a high-pitched voice at the same instant as a puff of light gray smoke blossomed from the muzzle of the heavy gun. But the warning was too late.

Tom and Seamus, jarred awake by the loud report of the big rifle, ran out on deck from their cabin. They had been sleeping in the bunk beds they shared with the other watch, making the most of their precious hours off duty. They looked down over the railing to the foredeck, horrified, as one of the young Irish deckhands lay sprawled, pumping great spouts of bright red blood onto the deck, his legs jittering and twitching as if he was trying to outrun the hexagonal forty-five caliber bullet that had just severed his aorta.

Tom and Seamus ran to the stairs along with the rest of the off-duty crew. They jumped down to the main deck and ran forward. They arrived where the boy was lying just as the engineer knelt in the broad slick of congealing blood to close the boy's staring, lifeless eyes. The boy's dungarees had a dark stain spreading in the crotch where his bladder had emptied. Seamus and Tom crossed themselves, both shivering in the cold rain.

Without thinking they, too, knelt beside the dead boy in the sticky pool of blood while all three of them began repeating the *Hail Mary* together in a sonorous monotone, barely audible above the thrumming of the engines behind them. As the towboat went on down the river, they left the sniper behind, still standing under his tree. They could see him casually begin to reload his rifle as he awaited another target of opportunity.

Later, as they went on deck to begin their watch, Seamus said quietly, "If we were passing that tree now, just an hour later, one of us could be lying there in a puddle of blood instead of that poor dead lad." He and Tom both crossed themselves again. It was October 31, Halloween, the day when many Irish people believed that the spirits of the recently deceased would pass among the living on their way to the other side.

With the strong flood pushing them along, they reached Johnsonville late that afternoon, having traveled downstream unencumbered by a tow at an average speed of seventeen miles per hour. While the crew were busy rounding up their empty coalboats and barges and rebuilding the tow for the trip back to Pittsburgh, Captain Sam went ashore to report to Colonel Thompson. The colonel was delighted to see Sam. He shook him warmly by the hand and congratulated him for surviving his dangerous mission.

"Just after you passed Florence, Captain Brown, some Confederate forces began crossing the river from South Florence, using the railway bridge. They ran into our troops under General Hatch, and after a short skirmish, Hatch retreated into Tennessee, thinking the rest of Hood's army was coming close behind. You must have just made it through Florence in the nick of time."

Sam shook his head in disbelief. "We seem to be pretty lucky, Colonel. I hope our luck lasts. Any sign of Forrest's cavalry since they occupied Fort Heiman, sir?"

"Neither hide nor hair, Captain. No transports have arrived here since you came, so we don't know if the rebs are still in the fort or not. Are you planning to go downriver?"

"I'll give it a try tonight, sir. I got past them in the dark on the way up here. Maybe I can do it again."

"You sure you don't want to wait 'til tomorrow? We're sending the transport *Venus* down with a gunboat escort."

"If it's all the same to you, Colonel, I'll take my chances in the dark. I don't want to be caught in the middle of a fight I didn't start."

Colonel Thompson laughed. "All right, Captain, have it your way. Are you ready to shove off?"

"We'll be heading home by nightfall, sir."

Midnight on Halloween night. This time the *Shark* and her tow were drifting slowly north with the current, hugging the eastern shore in the high water, the paddlewheel barely turning and all lights on board extinguished. It was still raining hard and there was no moon that night, so there would be no light at all to help the aim of the Confederate gunners. Captain Sam had warned the crew not to make the slightest sound as they neared the fort, just thirty-eight miles below Johnsonville.

Tom could hear sounds of activity coming from the fort as they passed by undetected in the dark. By the light of campfires and oil lanterns he could see Forrest's men hard at work. Their guns were being removed from the upper battery. Teams were being brought up and hitched to the guns and wagons, and teamsters were shouting and cursing at the horses and mules. Forrest's men would clearly be leaving Fort Heiman at the break of day, but where would they head this time, north or south?

Chapter Five

The *Shark's* destination was Brown's Station, next to the large estate owned by Captain Sam's father, William H. Brown. It was located at a beautiful wooded spot in a bend of the Monongahela River, across from Homestead, Pennsylvania, a few miles southeast of Pittsburgh. The beauty of the high wooded bluff overlooking the river was marred by the newly-built rail line passing at its foot and the coal yards and wharf boats strung out along the river. But that was a small price to pay for the mighty accumulation of Brown family wealth they represented.

Visitors could now arrive by train, get off at the little station by the river and be met by a carriage that would take them up a long, steep driveway cut into the side of Brown's Hill. At the top of the wooded bluff, a hundred and sixty feet above the river, they would reach "Rock Cottage", the Browns' private residence, where, far removed from the smoke and noise below, they could enjoy a view rivaling those of the valleys of the Hudson and the Delaware.

It was there that the *Shark* arrived early on Friday morning, the fourth of November, having taken three days and three nights to travel down the Tennessee from Johnsonville to Paducah and back up the Ohio to Pittsburgh, pushing her tow of empties. Tom had gone out on deck at four o'clock, before the sun was up, to begin his watch. As they passed the pretty little river town of Sewickley, the sun broke through the scattered clouds above the hilltops to the northeast, sending golden rays across the river through the moisture-laden air.

Thank God, thought Tom, no more rain. Downing the last of his coffee, he returned the empty mug to the cook house and went forward to take up his watch station at the front of the tow. He liked the morning watches the best of all, the peace and quiet of the fresh new day beginning. And today he would go home for the weekend to his parents and sisters.

They traveled another fifteen miles up the Ohio to the Point and into the mouth of the shallow Monongahela, its banks crowded with riverboats of all kinds. Avoiding islands, sandbars and two bridges, they went on upstream past Pittsburgh and Hazelwood before rounding the big bend in the river to reach Brown's Station.

Captain Sam's father had worried about him during his absence, scouring the pages of the Pittsburgh *Gazette* each morning for news of the fighting on the Tennessee. He was already waiting on the wharf as the *Shark* landed, and he came aboard to greet his son.

"Sam, thank God you're safe. But how the hell did you manage to get here? We just got news that Forrest's cavalry attacked and captured the transport *Venus* and the *Undine,* her navy gunboat escort, a little way downriver from Johnsonville. They apparently mounted two of their field guns on the *Venus* and turned her into a goddamned Confederate cavalry gunboat. The two boats raised hell with the traffic on the river for days until two other navy gunboats came down from Johnsonville and recaptured the *Venus.* The rebels abandoned and burned the *Undine* and got away on land with all their weapons and horses. Where was the *Shark* while all this was going on?"

Sam recounted the story of their two midnight escapades, adding that before leaving Johnsonville he had fortunately turned down an offer to be part of the *Venus's* convoy.

"You must be the luckiest man on the river, son. But don't stretch your luck too far. You've had more than your share already."

Tom invited Seamus Kelly to come home with him for the weekend. He knew his parents and sisters would enjoy meeting the young Irishman, who would probably relish a home-cooked Irish Sunday dinner, having no family of his own on this side of the Atlantic. And maybe he and Mary might even take a liking to each other.

So it was that, once they had seen the *Shark* safely moored for the weekend at Brown's Station and caught a ride up the Mon on a Brown's pool boat, the two bunkmates walked across the old covered bridge to the Malone house in West Brownsville, carrying Seamus' gift for Tom's parents, a large newspaper-wrapped catfish for Friday night supper. The young men (and the fish) were welcomed with open arms and shouts of joy by Jack, Margaret and the three girls, who, having earlier heard the alarming war news from the South, had feared the worst for Tom and his comrades.

While Margaret and Mary made supper ready at the little kitchen table, Tom described their adventures on the Tennessee River in dramatic terms. "There we was, Da, Seamus and me, rowing Captain Sam up the river into battle in a sixteen-foot yawl boat without any guns. I was thinking of you and yer own Da back in Ireland on yer little ferry. Except nobody was shooting at you then, was they?"

Jack Malone laughed, pleased that Tom still remembered his earlier career as a ferryman with his own father back in Ireland. "If they was, son, we'd have rowed hard in the other direction. But don't forget, Tom, yer Grandpa Edward Malone was no coward. Sure, and didn't me Da fight Napoleon wit' the Duke of Wellington at Waterloo fifty years ago, so he did."

Embarrassed at hearing his father's oft-repeated claim yet again, Tom tried to exchange looks with Seamus. But Seamus was not looking in his direction. Seamus was totally engaged in watching Mary Malone as she moved about the kitchen quickly and efficiently, helping her mother to prepare supper. Mary was well aware of the rapt attention she was receiving from the visitor, and her round face reddened as she worked away, occasionally granting Seamus a shy, sidelong smile.

Margaret tried to break the spell her daughter was casting and draw Seamus into the conversation. "And what about yer own family, Mister Kelly? Any soldiers there?"

Seamus reddened too at being put suddenly in the limelight. "Ah, well, yes indeed, Missis Malone. Me grandfather fought at Boolavogue with Father Murphy back in '98, and…" Here Seamus hesitated and looked down at his hands, tears welling from his eyes. "And me own Da was killed by the Rooshins at Balaclava, ma'am, just ten years ago this past week." He raised a hand to wipe away his tears.

Mary could not help herself. She placed her own hand tenderly on Seamus' shoulder as she turned to her mother. "Mam, let's ask Father Heaney to include Mister Kelly's father in his prayers on Sunday. Will we do that? Will we, Mam?"

Ireland had long been known as "the land of saints and scholars". Indeed, Irish martyrologies listed literally hundreds of saints. To avoid neglecting somebody's local favorite, the Irish Church had solemnized November 6 each year as a blanket feast honoring *all* the Irish saints, too numerous to mention, starting with Saint Patrick.

Irish immigrant communities in other countries tried to keep this tradition alive in their new homes as best they could, and, on that Sunday morning, by coincidence November 6, a large crowd, mainly Irish born or of Irish descent, climbed the steep hill toward St. Peter's Church in Brownsville to attend a special High Mass to be celebrated by Father Heaney.

The Malone family, accompanied by Seamus Kelly, were among the throng of worshippers that day. As a memorial for the tenth anniversary of his father's death, Seamus had made a special offering to the church the day before. Father Heaney had in turn offered to pray for the repose of the elder Kelly's soul and to have him remembered at the altar during the Mass.

Leaving the church after the Mass, Seamus gallantly offered his arm to Mary as they descended the icy steps to the street. She proudly accepted, smiling at Seamus and hoping her friends would notice them walking down the hill together. Tom quietly congratulated himself for bringing Seamus home with him for the weekend. Maybe Mary had found a beau at last. Perhaps his stalwart friend had sensed her finer qualities, for surely she would make a wonderful wife for any lucky man. Tom decided to do his best to promote a match between them.

Mary had baked an apple pie for dessert. Seamus was enchanted. "Ach, Miss Mary, Sure,'tis the most delicious pie I ever tasted in all me born days. Ye're a brilliant cook, that ye are."

Mary beamed. Tom was already thinking of arranging another meeting between the two when Seamus, with a crumb of pie crust lodged in his shaggy red beard, suddenly turned to Tom's parents and spoke up. "Mister and Missis Malone, *go raibh míle maith agat.* Thank you a thousand times for the wonderful weekend. And I especially enjoyed meeting Miss Mary. May I have your permission to write to her and to call on her again when I am back here in Brownsville?"

Jack Malone tried hard to remain calm as he replied. "*Cinnte.* Yes, indeed, Mister Kelly, *cead míle fáilte.* Ye're most welcome to call here any time."

Shocking news from war correspondents assigned with Thomas's troops in Nashville reached Pittsburgh the following week. The men of the *Shark* were horrified to learn from newspaper reports that, after the *Venus* had been recaptured by the Union gunboats and the small Confederate "navy" had abandoned and burned the *Undine*, they had headed upriver with their two salvaged artillery pieces and rejoined Forrest's main force of only three thousand men, dug in and concealed that night in the woods just across the river from Johnsonville.

On Friday, the 4th of November, the same day the *Shark* had arrived in Brown's Station, the Johnsonville depot had been a busy place, with three gunboats, eleven transports, and eighteen barges docked there; and two trains on the sidings, being loaded from the many warehouses. Forrest's gunners had waited patiently until the opportune moment that afternoon when all the men and supplies were assembled across the river from their hiding place. Then, at half past three, all the Confederate guns went off at once, disabling the Federal gunboats.

Caught by surprise, Colonel Thompson and Lieutenant King, the commander of the small naval force, believed incorrectly that their two thousand men, many of them "colored troops," were badly outnumbered. They thought that the Confederates, believed to number over thirteen thousand, would come across the river and capture their gunboats and transports to help Hood cross the river. They set all the boats on fire to prevent them from falling into enemy hands.

Carried by the wind, the fire quickly spread to the warehouses while the artillery duel continued across the river. In the confusion, the stationmaster headed east with a train loaded with supplies and four hundred men, some of whom later looted the supplies. The boxcars were abandoned at Waverly, and the engine and tender went on to Nashville, seventy-eight miles to the east.

The fires burned through the night, providing enough illumination for most of Forrest's men to withdraw six miles to the south. An artillery detachment left behind as a rear guard continued shelling the smoldering ruins of Johnsonville the next morning. Five days later, Forrest and his men were once again safely back in Corinth, Mississippi with a hundred fifty Union prisoners.

He had lost only two of his men, with nine others wounded. The Union had lost eight men killed or wounded, four gunboats, fourteen transports, seventeen barges, thirty-two guns, the men taken prisoner and over seventy-five thousand tons of supplies, worth almost seven million dollars.

Forrest's raid into West Tennessee had created near panic in the North, and one report even had him near Chicago with fourteen thousand men. A few months later, Lee surrendered, Lincoln was assassinated and the war finally ended.

Chapter Six: 1866

On September 20, Brown's Line sold the four-year-old *Shark* to the Mississippi Valley Transportation Company in St. Louis. The "MVT" bought a few surplus towboats and barges after the war ended and were pioneering in the rapidly growing bulk grain trade between St. Louis and New Orleans. Tom and Seamus went downriver from Pittsburgh with an unusual late September flood to help deliver the *Shark* and her last tow of coal before she was taken over by the new owners. They stayed on with the MVT aboard the *Shark* for the rest of the winter and on into the spring of 1867, enjoying the warmer weather on the Lower Mississippi but growing increasingly homesick for Pennsylvania and their loved ones.

Seamus Kelly and Mary Malone had become engaged to be married just before he and Tom went downriver. Seamus and Mary were both saving their money until they could have enough to buy a home together. Still earning fifty dollars a month, Seamus decided to stay on the *Shark* for the long, hot summer. He figured he and Mary could put aside enough money to get married in the fall, and so they set a date in the following September for a wedding at St. Peter's in Brownsville. They corresponded faithfully, writing long, loving letters to each other each week throughout the winter, spring and summer and waiting for September to come. Tom, who had agreed to be Seamus' best man, was happy to keep him company on the *Shark* and save some money of his own.

Summer on the Lower Missippi was usually a time of sickness, mostly endemic malaria and dysentery, with periodic outbreaks of cholera and yellow fever, particularly among the immigrant population, who had no acquired immunity to the diseases. Tom learned that a major yellow fever epidemic had hit New Orleans in the summer of 1853, killing thousands. He always felt relieved whenever the *Shark* would deliver her wheat and head back upriver again to St. Louis with empty barges for a new tow.

In August, the two bunkmates finally decided to leave the *Shark* in St. Louis on their next trip upriver and make their way back to Brownsville. The *Shark* left New Orleans just as the first summer yellow fever cases were being reported there. Sulfur and tar fires were burning on street corners in the belief that the foul-smelling smoke would chase the disease away. Many of the better-off citizens had already left the city to get away from the spread of the fever, leaving behind mainly the black population and the many Irish immigrants.

The *Shark* passed Memphis a day later without stopping. That afternoon Seamus felt ill during his watch on deck. Apologizing to Tom, he stumbled back to his berth to lie down. A few hours later, when Tom finished his watch, he found his friend burning with fever. Seamus shook with chills, his heartbeat rapid. He complained of nausea, headache, back pains, and weakness.

The *Shark* immediately turned back downriver to Memphis, and Seamus was carried ashore to receive medical care, with Tom to accompany him. Two days later in a hospital ward, Seamus developed jaundice, his ruddy complexion and bright eyes turning yellow. After the third day his symptoms receded, only to return again with a terrible vengeance a day later. In the last stage, he began vomiting thick, black blood and lapsed into delirium and finally a coma. Less than a week after leaving New Orleans, Seamus Kelly was dead.

Tom trudged slowly, his head down, as he approached the long covered bridge to West Brownsville a week later. After the hurried burial of Seamus Kelly's remains in a grave in Memphis, he had decided to carry the awful news to poor Mary himself, rather than sending her a telegram. Memphis had not yet been quarantined, so he was able to get deck space on a packet for Pittsburgh, where he changed to a Monongahela River steamboat for the short trip to Brownsville, dreading the sad task that awaited him there.

He found his father on duty in the tollhouse. Jack Malone greeted his son with a happy cry, "Glory be to God, 'tis himself, back from the river." But, as he saw the look on Tom's face, his own expression changed suddenly. "But where's Seamus? Where's the bridegroom? Don't ye be telling me he's got cold feet, now."

Tom could no longer control his grief. He broke down completely, sobbing like a child. "Oh, Da. Seamus is dead. Yellow fever it was. He caught it in New Orleans just as we were leaving to come home. I buried poor Seamus in Memphis, Da. How are we ever going to tell our Mary?"

"Pull yerself together, boy. Don't let Mary see ye blubbering like a baby. Just go home now and get all the girls together and sit them down before ye say anything."

Tom shuddered, pulled out a handkerchief and wiped his eyes and blew his nose. He straightened up and, without another word to his father but with a desolate expression on his face, set out walking into the dark tunnel of the covered bridge toward the house across the river where poor Mary was waiting for her lost bridegroom.

When Tom told her the news, Mary went pale and jerked as if she had been struck in the face. She then murmured, "Dear Jesus, Tom. What an awful time you must have had."

How typical of Mary, Tom thought. Always putting the cares of others ahead of her own. He watched her as she excused herself, took her Rosary beads out of the apron pocket where she always kept them, and went outside to the back yard to be alone with her grief.

Margaret came right to the point, "Did poor Seamus leave any money, Tom? I know he and Mary were saving to buy a house."

"Yes, Mam, he did. Before he died, he asked me to send the money to his mother back in Ireland."

Margaret frowned. "What about our Mary, Tom? In a few weeks she would have been his wife. Don't ye think she'd be entitled to the money?"

"I can't do that, Mam. I promised him. He gave me his mother's address. And I have to tell her the news. She doesn't know yet."

"Surely we could keep part of it for Mary. His mother would never know. How much is there anyway, Tom?"

Tom's anger flared. "That's none of your damned business."

Margaret swung her arm to slap his face, but he caught her by the wrist. "I'll be twenty-one in a few weeks, Mam. I won't be slapped in the face like a child any more ... not by you, not by anyone."

In early October, Tom carefully packed the new Bible he had just received from Father Heaney on his twenty-first birthday, September 29, 1867. The date was inscribed inside the cover together with an Irish blessing written by the priest. He kissed his mother and his sisters good-bye, picked up his bag and headed back across the river to find a new job.

With the fall rains, the Monongahela River was slowly inching up on the flood gauge by the bridge as he stopped at the toll house to say goodbye to his father. October seemed to be the month of parting for Tom, as a riverman on the Ohio. It was the month when the fall harvest was finished on the little farms along the river and steamboat owners started hiring their crews again to prepare for the winter navigation season. A year had passed since he and Seamus had traveled downriver together to St. Louis to deliver the *Shark* to the MVT, a year of radical changes, riots and massacres in southern cities, where martial law still ruled.

While Tom was away with the *Shark*, Peter Malone had come home from the war a changed man. For more than two years his cavalry company had been assigned to routine guard duty on the railroad and patrolling in the Upper Potomac around Romney,

Moorefield and Petersburg, far from the battlefields. Company D had lost only three men in action, while nineteen had died of disease. With little real fighting and many days of boredom, his military service had left him bitter and frustrated. His dreams of glory, leading charges on horseback against the Confederate guns with his saber drawn and bloodied, were never realized. Instead, never promoted above the rank of private, he had learned to drink whiskey and play cards. Tom understood why he had hardly written any letters home during the war.

Pete didn't stay long in the little house in Brownsville with his parents and sisters, but preferred to spend most of his time in Pittsburgh where life was more exciting. Tom saw him occasionally, but their old camaraderie was gone. It was almost as if Tom, not Pete, was now the "big brother" of the family.

Tom was finally "free, white and twenty-one" and had earned the right to claim a slightly higher monthly salary as an experienced deckhand. He could also vote in the next election if he chose to. A serious young man, Tom often pondered such things, and he found himself doing so as he walked through the long, dark bridge, heading for the pool at the Alicia coal tipple to catch a ride down to Brown's Station.

When he arrived in Pittsburgh later that day, he found a new Brown's Line towboat waiting. She was the *Sam Brown,* named by the family to honor their own war hero and eldest son. She had been built in McKeesport only the year before, just 334 tons displacement, or about two-thirds the size of the *Shark.* But she was powerful, built for speed, with twenty-inch pistons and an eight-foot stroke, fed by four big boilers. She was designed to travel through the water at speeds upward from seven miles an hour.

Tom went aboard and found the captain, a young Irishman named Mike Dougherty, entering the day's weather data in the log on the dining table. Captain Mike had come over from Ireland to Pittsburgh in '56 at the age of twenty-four. Now, at thirty-five, he was a captain with his first command. He already had a nodding acquaintance with Tom, and he knew the story of the *Shark's* heroic midnight escapades and ascent of the Muscle Shoals rapids during the flood of '64 on the Tennessee.

"Sure, Tom, I'll give ye a job. I need an experienced hand like you to keep an eye on the young spalpeens I had to hire last winter when we launched the *Sam Brown*. A lot of Irish lads turned up in Pittsburgh after the war. The army taught 'em how to drill and fight well enough, but most o' them are landsmen whose only voyage on water was coming across the sea from Ireland."

"How much can you pay, Captain?"

"How does sixty dollars sound, Tom?"

"Where do I sign, Captain Mike?" Tom was relieved to be getting back on the river again and away from Brownsville. The past month had been painful, the tension between him and his parents upsetting the whole family.

Captain Mike opened the payroll ledger and held out the pen he had been using. Tom signed. "Where do I bunk?"

"I'll put ye in the after cabin, across from the laundry, Tom. It's a little quieter than the other one opposite the firemen and strikers. That suit ye?"

"When do we leave here, Captain?"

"When the Mon gives us another foot or so of water, we'll start building our tow. In the meantime, ye can touch up the paint on deck. Oh, and see to the yawl boat too, Tom."

"Yes sir, Captain. Thank you, sir." Tom touched his cap and headed aft to the crew's quarters to find his cabin and stow his belongings.

Tom's new bunkmate was another young Irish immigrant who, unlike Seamus, had enlisted in the Union Army the moment his feet touched land in Philadelphia, overwhelmed by the offer of thirteen dollars a month, three meals a day, a musket, an overcoat and a brand new blue uniform. John Murray, from County Cavan, told Tom he had served as a private in Company D of the 69th Pennsylvania—the "Irish Volunteers." He fought at Gettysburg, somehow surviving the bloodbath of Pickett's charge, but was later wounded at Spotsylvania Court House on

May 12, 1864. He mustered out on September 10 that year, at the expiration of his enlistment. His regiment had lost half of its men— killed, wounded or captured— at Gettysburg alone.

John was a little older than Tom, about the same age as Pete, Tom thought. He had the same wiry build as Pete, too, but what a difference in their war experiences. He had the same rakish good looks as Pete, but his hair and beard were black like Tom's, framing a pair of bright blue eyes.

As he and Tom worked aboard the *Sam Brown,* touching up the paint on the bulwarks and railings, John told Tom that he had left Philadelphia after the war and headed west on the railroad to Pittsburgh, looking for work. Philadelphia had been overflowing with poor Irish immigrants, John said, and there had been violent clashes between the Irish slum-dwellers and the "Know-nothings" as far back as '44.

"I had me mustering-out pay in me pocket, Tom, and me blue uniform on me back, so I hopped a freight car that carried me to Pittsburgh, a fine place with more jobs and more room to grow."

John explained that, like other Irishmen, he had found cheap accommodation in the shanty town atop Pittsburgh's Hill District, which had also received an influx of freed slaves following the war. One such person, a young woman who had been a house slave and cook, worked at a boarding house on Wylie Avenue, catering to newcomers of all descriptions. She and John eventually shared a living arrangement and had two children together. Tom was astonished by John's openness about this relationship. Mixed-race couples were a rarity, even in the North.

During the summers of low water in the river, John easily found construction work in the rapidly growing city. In the winter navigation season, when construction slowed, he found work on the river. All in all, he said, he could not complain … he was a very happy man. He was grateful to have survived so many battles with only a "wee scar" from a Confederate Minie ball, which had miraculously passed through his leg without breaking bones or severing arteries, leaving him with a slight limp but with use of both legs.

Most of the paintwork was done when, a few weeks later, cold autumn rains raised the Monongahela River high enough for the *Sam Brown* to head downriver. Tom and John gladly put away their buckets and paint brushes and started assembling the first tow.

Chapter Seven: 1870

The Ohio crested at over fifty-five feet in Cincinnati on January 19, much earlier than usual. The river had been gradually rising ever since late August, and the Line's towboats had been as busy as beavers, pushing record tonnages of coal downriver all that winter, taking advantage of the early start of navigation and the near record flood that followed.

Tom Malone, twenty-three years old and just promoted to watchman on the *Sam Brown,* seldom had time to visit his family that winter. He and the mate divided the six-hour watches between them, each having the same responsibility for the day-to-day operation of the boat and the handling of the tow and each reporting directly to Captain Mike or the pilot when on duty.

The mate, Ad Sykes, had learned his job for three years as a watchman and had also just been promoted. A tough, jovial riverman, he had served on a navy gunboat during the war and had met Captain Sam as a shipmate. After mustering out, he had come straight upriver to Brown's Station to pay his respects and offer his services. Captain Sam had hired him and assigned him to Captain Mike as watchman on the *Sam Brown.*

Now that Ad and Tom were standing opposite watches, they hardly ever saw each other outside the dining room, where they handed over the watch to each other every six hours. While one was on deck the other was usually in his cabin sleeping or relaxing. During his first two years on the *Sam Brown,* though, Tom had stood Ad's watches, and the two men had learned to like and respect each other.

Tom loved having his own watchman's cabin in the officers' quarters. Though he was very fond of John Murray, the Irishman had snored loudly, often interfering with Tom's sleep. Sometimes, also, Murray had awakened suddenly from terrifying nightmares, reliving his battlefield experiences, and had attacked Tom in his upper berth before coming to his senses and realizing what he was doing.

Now John was standing Tom's watches, putting in the time he needed to earn a promotion of his own. They often talked about Ireland during quiet nights on the river. Tom's parents had told him very little about their own Irish origins, and he was curious to learn more.

He had heard from his parents that they had been illiterate, landless laborers. He knew that his father and grandfather had found work as ferrymen, carrying passengers across some Irish river for a few cents each way. Jack and Margaret had told Tom that they had not married until the week before leaving Cork to sail to America, arriving in New York in 1842. He knew that Da's older sisters, Katie and Eliza Malone, had come over earlier, getting jobs as housemaids in Pittsburgh. But beyond these few facts, Tom knew nothing about his Irish family.

He wished he had been more inquisitive as a child. His Da was usually away from home working, but he had spent many hours with his mother, and he might have asked her more questions about Ireland. He was always glad whenever he and John Murray could while away a quiet hour on the river with John's tales of his youth back in County Cavan.

"Ach, life was dog rough back there, Tom, that it was. Cavan suffered more than most during the Hunger. When me Mam died in '47, I was fostered out to her brother, who worked me half to death. We lived on praties when we could get 'em and on prayers when we couldn't."

He explained how, like Tom's parents, he had been helped to emigrate by an older sister who had found work as a maid in

Philadelphia. When he arrived there in the summer of '61, he was met by recruiters on the dock who told him that they were forming an Irish regiment to defend America's capital. "And the rest is history, like they say."

"Do you ever want to go back there to visit, John?"

"Now why would I ever want to be doing that, Tom? I'm as happy as a clam here in America. This is my home now. Going back to Ireland? It makes me feel sad just to think about it."

Tom wondered if his parents felt the same way.

As spring arrived and the winter snow melted and passed on down into the Mississippi and the Gulf of Mexico, the waters of the Ohio gradually receded. But fortunes were being made in the Pittsburgh coal trade that year, and boat owners wanted to keep shipping coal as long as possible, while avoiding leaving their towboats and barges stranded downstream.

They believed that, if they could still get their tow downriver over the shoals at Letart Falls, two hundred and thirty-five miles below Pittsburgh, they would still have enough time to deliver their coal and bring the empties back to Pittsburgh before low water finally forced an end to the navigation season.

The *Sam Brown* had nearly grounded her tow at Letart Falls on the way down to Cincinnati in early July. Loaded, her tow drew nine feet, while the boat herself drew only five. Tom knew it would be their last trip of the summer as they arrived in Cincinnati, delivered the coal and picked up a tow of empties. He was exhausted, having worked steadily since September, and he was looking forward to a good rest back home in Brownsville. Later he might find a little work with Bill Walsh at the boatyard while he was waiting for the next navigation season to begin.

As the *Sam Brown* pushed her empties upriver past the mouth of the Kanawha River at Point Pleasant, West Virginia, Tom and Captain Mike suddenly realized that there was no more barge traffic coming toward them down the Upper Ohio, only a few small craft. They feared that they might be too late to get past Letart Falls. They kept going slowly upriver for another twenty-five miles, carefully sounding the depth as they went, past Pomeroy and Racine on the Ohio side. There was hardly any current left in the river. They had finally reached low water, and there was no point in trying to go any farther.

Captain Mike found a good, safe mooring spot for his tow on the Ohio side of the river near the mouth of Yellowbush Creek, halfway between the town of Racine and the little village of Antiquity. After running the tow into the shallow water beside the broad expanse of exposed river bottom near the mouth of the creek, he cast off the tow and backed the *Sam Brown* out into the channel again.

They steamed a mile farther upriver and docked at the landing in Antiquity, which was already accumulating stranded riverboats. Captain Mike went into town to get permission to leave the boat there until the water would rise enough for him to take her and the empties over Letart Falls and back to Pittsburgh in the fall.

Captain Mike assembled his officers in the dining room and made an offer to them. "Which o' yez wants to stay here in Antiquity and take care of the boat? The Browns'll pay yer full salary and enough to cover yer vittles. Ye just have to keep the boat and the tow in good repair. The rest of us'll walk across the bend to the Apple Grove landing and catch a packet back to Pittsburgh."

Tom was the only officer on the *Sam Brown* without dependents waiting for him back home. "I guess I can stay here, Captain. I'll write a letter to my folks in Brownsville and tell 'em I'm down here earning lots o' money."

"Fine, Tom, I was hoping you'd take the job. Antiquity don't look so bad. Seems like a nice little place. Plenty of fresh meat and produce."

"Is there a Catholic church around here, Captain? I'm a regular Mass goer back home."

"Afraid not, Tom. Sure, there's lots of us micks out here on the riverboats, but not many living in these little towns. That change yer mind, does it?"

"Naw, I guess not, Captain. I've got my Bible and my beads. I'll be all right I guess."

"Sure ye will, Tom. Good man on ye."

The next morning at sunup the rest of the crew packed their belongings and left for Apple Grove, a small landing above the falls, about a four-mile walk from Antiquity. Captain Mike carried a letter for Tom's parents. Tom soon found himself alone, except for a few friendly, curious local visitors who were anxious to come aboard and inspect the fast, powerful Brown's Line towboat.

Two of Tom's visitors said they were actually rivermen themselves, two of the handful of rivermen living there in Antiquity. Albert and George Powell were brothers, aged twenty-one and nineteen. Albert had served the last year of the war in the navy on Mississippi River gunboats and then worked on steam engines in the gas and oil fields of West Virginia, while George had hired on as a deckhand on a country packet at eighteen, just like Tom.

The Powell brothers told Tom that they spent their summers helping their widowed mother run a small truck farm on a strip of rich bottom land along the river just north of town; the spring floods deposited silt there each year, they said, replenishing the fertility and moisture of the soil.

Tom observed the two brothers as he showed them around the *Sam Brown's* boilers and engine room. Albert, the more serious of the two, seemed delighted by their modern design and asked Tom many questions, some of which he was unable to answer, not being an engineer himself.

George, like Tom, was more interested in the *Sam Brown's* exterior, especially the four big "towing knees" on her bow, designed for pushing the heavy loaded barges. He asked Tom a lot of questions about the daily tasks of the deckhands on a towboat.

"Most of their work is out on the tow rather than on the boat." Tom explained.

"Seems like a lot tougher job than what we do on the packets, Tom. Maybe more dangerous, too."

"I guess maybe you're right, George" Tom couldn't help feeling a sense of pride at this admission. He liked this young man's candor and humility.

Their tour ended, the Powell brothers thanked their host and invited him to pay a return visit to their farm whenever he liked. "Why don't you come next Sunday after church, Tom?" asked George. "Our mother and sister will cook you a real good dinner."

"All right. Thanks a lot. That sounds grand. How will I find your place?"

"Why don't you just meet us after church? Antiquity Baptist is the only church in town, so you can't miss it." George replied easily, not realizing that Tom was a Catholic – a rarity in those parts – who might have serious qualms about attending a Baptist service.

Tom hesitated, then agreed, "Okay then, see you boys on Sunday."

The two brothers crossed the gangplank, turning to wave to Tom before walking up the narrow dirt road leading to their farm. Tom was alone. He went to his cabin and took out his Bible and rosary beads, troubled by the thought of attending a Baptist church service. He hoped he would be forgiven.

Chapter Eight

Tom had never set foot in a Protestant church. He had been taught that it was a sin for him to go to one, that he could even be excommunicated for doing it, that he would have to confess it the next time he went home. But he never missed church on Sunday unless he was actually traveling on the river and thus entitled to a traveler's dispensation. He loved the feeling of God's presence he had during the Mass. The thought of spending the next three or four months without once hearing a sermon, singing a hymn or joining others in prayer seemed even worse to him than the sin he was about to commit.

Throughout his childhood he had heard stories from his parents and their friends about the persecution and eviction of Catholics by their Protestant landlords in Ireland, and he knew that, even in America, Protestant "Orangemen" and native-born American "Know-nothings" had been stirring up anti-Catholic violence in the eastern cities since before he was born.

And, just before leaving Cincinnati, Tom had heard that eight people had been killed in New York City when outraged Catholics protested during the annual July 12 Boyne Day march, held by Protestant Irish Orangemen to celebrate the victory of Prince William of Orange over Catholic King James II at the Battle of the Boyne in 1690. Tom had felt ashamed of the Catholic rioters. America was a free country, and, if the Orangemen wanted to march on the Twelfth, they should be allowed to do so and not be attacked by a mob of drunken hooligans.

On Sunday morning he washed his face and hands, trimmed his beard and moustache, made a pot of coffee and fried some eggs and bacon. After cleaning up the dishes, he read from his Bible and put on his best clothes to go to meet the Powell brothers at the little Baptist church.

He didn't know what to expect. Should he take his Rosary beads with him as he usually did when going to Mass? He fidgeted with them nervously and then tucked them away in his pocket. He put on his cap and went ashore after carefully locking the doors to the cabins on the main deck.

The little wooden church was tucked against a hillside across the road from the river, safe from the all but the highest floodwaters. Tom searched the small crowd of worshipers gathered outside, looking for the Powell brothers. He saw them waiting there with an elderly couple, a middle-aged woman and a young girl. The latter two bore a very strong resemblance to each other, and Tom felt sure they were mother and daughter.

The girl noticed him and smiled shyly, taking Tom's breath away for an instant. She looked fresh-faced, innocent and engaging, as if she welcomed every new experience and each new person she met. Reddish brown ringlets peeked from underneath her prim bonnet, and a light sprinkling of summer freckles set off her twinkling blue eyes, which looked at him evenly from either side of a long, straight nose. When she smiled, little dimples appeared around the corners of her mouth.

Although Tom was not good at guessing women's ages, he thought she must be about the same age as his sister Ellen, sixteen or seventeen. Under her high-necked "Sunday best" bodice, he was aware of a firm young figure, and he felt a sudden impious stirring in his loins as he imagined what beauty might be concealed there.

George Powell approached and took him by the arm, leading him back toward the little group. "Folks, this here is Tom Malone, the watchman on the *Sam Brown*. Tom, these are my grandparents, Mr. and Mrs. Varian, my mother, Mrs. Powell, and my sister, Roxanne. We call her Roxa."

"Mighty pleased to meet you, folks. And thanks for inviting me. It's kind of lonely staying on the boat all by myself."

"You're most welcome, young man." Mrs. Powell replied, taking Tom's arm and leading him toward the door. "Let's go in and find our places. The worship service is about to begin."

Full of misgivings, his heart pounding, Tom entered the little wooden building, very conscious of the fact that he was deliberately going against the teachings of Rome and his parents, walking into a forbidden Protestant church. He was surprised to discover, however, once he was inside and seated in a pew, that he felt lighter and happier, suddenly free of the strict rules of his childhood. And he was enjoying the company of the Powell family, especially being near Roxa, who had somehow managed to sit next to him in the pew.

As the service began, Tom was surprised to see that many of the worshipers had brought their own Bibles with them. Catholics, he knew, were not encouraged by their church to read the Bible themselves. Rather, it was reserved for the priests to explain the meaning of the selected daily scriptures in their homilies. Tom, however, had become an eager Bible scholar in spite of this tradition and had read the "Good Book" from cover to cover more than once during long hours spent on the river.

Tom liked the "Gospel" singing during the service and gladly lent his clear baritone voice to the hymns, a few of which were already familiar to him. The music had an authentic American ring to it that seemed to him more appropriate than the Latin prayers and chants he was used to at St. Peter's. As the service came to an end, everyone joined in singing "Amazing Grace," an English hymn treasured by the abolitionist movement and one of Tom's very favorites. The little wooden church resounded to the sweet, lilting harmony of the old hymn.

On the way out, the Powells introduced Tom to the pastor, "Brother" Conyers, who had given a rousing sermon about the devil and the temptations of Christ. Tom was pleasantly surprised by the custom of addressing Baptist pastors as "brother". So many differences. And he liked all of them. The pastor greeted him warmly and asked him to come back for a covered-dish supper on Wednesday evening. Tom, already tired of eating his own cooking, accepted gratefully.

Brother Conyers beamed at Tom and winked at the Powells, already anticipating the addition of a new member to his small flock. The group bade the pastor farewell and headed north along the river bank to the little Powell farmhouse where Sunday dinner awaited them.

Tom was impressed when they reached the farm. It was a marvel of compactness, running down a grassy slope between the hill and the water's edge and straddling a bend in the narrow dirt road north of the village. It could not have been more than a couple of acres. In back of the house, Mrs. Powell kept chickens and a pig. There was a smokehouse, a springhouse, a wash house and a small barn. Between the house and the road was a vegetable garden, and behind the house, running down to the river, was a low-water pasture and a corn field. Across the road, another pasture ran a little way up the hill and into the woods. Not an inch of space was wasted.

As they approached the house, Tom could smell the aroma of roast chicken and fresh baked bread. He had not eaten a home cooked meal for many weeks, and his mouth began to water as he imagined the feast that awaited them.

Dinner at the Powell farm was a festive, jolly affair, very different, Tom thought, from the silent meals in the Malone house in West Brownsville. They began the meal with a lengthy prayer of thanks and blessing offered by Grandpa Varian, who thanked the Creator for, among other things, stranding Tom's towboat in Antiquity for the summer and bringing him to their home as a guest. Lively conversation flowed around the table as the family dug into a huge feast of roast chicken, garnished with fresh garden vegetables and potatoes grown on the rich alluvial soil of the little farm.

Tom sat between Mrs. Powell and her mother, Hannah Dunn Varian, who told Tom that her parents, like his, had been poor Irish immigrants, arriving in America just after the Revolution, part of a large exodus of "non-conformists" from the Irish province of Ulster in the late 1700's.

"Though I was actually born in New York City, Tom, we came here from Washington County, Pennsylvania, more than fifty years ago. I met Mr. Varian here and married him in 1820. He was a cooper then. He and I were married on the 12th of July, of all days, in another Baptist church in Letart, Virginia, just across the river."

"Why, I grew up in Washington County too, ma'am. Ain't it a small world?" marveled Tom, helping himself to the mashed potatoes.

During the meal he exchanged frequent looks with Roxa, who seemed pleased by his attention. She smiled at him often, showing her dimples with a little upward twist of her mouth that verged on a look of amusement. Could she be making fun of him? He wondered. After all, he was nearly seven years her senior, and he had seen a good bit of the world. She had probably never ventured farther from home than the county seat at Pomeroy, ten miles downriver.

As if sensing his musing, she suddenly turned to him and asked, "Were you in the war, Mr. Malone? My brother Albert was down on the Mississippi in '64."

"Please call me Tom, Miss Powell. Yes, I did see a little action on the Tennessee River that year. We were running charters out of Pittsburgh for the Quartermaster's Department."

"Oh, please tell us about your adventures, Tom. And please call me Roxa. Everyone does."

Tom relaxed, instantly put at ease by her friendly invitation. She did not seem to be the least bit shy, nor did she seem to be making fun of him.

"Well, in late October of '64 we were towing coal to the navy up in Tennessee and even as far as Alabama..." he began, launching into an animated account of Captain Sam's daredevil exploits, their climbing the rapids at Muscle Shoals, his seeing "Sherman's hairpins" on the demolished railway in Decatur and their two narrow midnight escapes by sneaking under Forrest's guns. He was not a bad storyteller, and the family listened attentively, asking questions from time to time. All the while, a pair of twinkling blue eyes were smiling at him.

Tom thought often about Roxa as he puttered about on the *Brown* the following three days, making small repairs, cleaning, polishing and painting. When Wednesday finally came around, he was eager to go to the church supper, hoping that she would be there too. He washed and put on clean clothes, carefully combing his hair and beard and humming one of the Gospel tunes he had heard on Sunday as he surveyed himself in the looking glass. He was not bad looking, he thought, a little shaggy perhaps. No time to find a barber, though. He didn't want to arrive late to the supper and draw too much attention.

Horses and wagons were drawn up outside the church. Men were smoking and talking outside as the women uncovered their dishes on the wooden picnic tables and prepared to serve the supper. Tom greeted the Powell boys and their grandfather and was introduced in turn to a group of their friends and neighbors, always curious to meet any newcomers to their tiny village from the outside world.

Tom noticed that several of the men had limbs missing, empty coat sleeves or trouser legs pinned up. George Powell had been loudly recounting Tom's story of the previous Sunday, and he continued, laughing, "Yeah, and then they snuck right past old Bedford Forrest's guns in the dark. The secesh gunners never even knowed they was there."

One of the veterans, a one-legged man with a long beard, leaning on a crutch, spat a yellow jet of tobacco juice near Tom's feet and drawled, "Well, ain't you the lucky one. We met Forrest and his boys up in Franklin, Tennessee, in broad daylight, and ain't nobody done no sneaking there. We stood and fought them damn rebs all day long. Kilt more than five thousand of 'em, too."

Tom flushed with embarrassment and stammered, "No sir, what we done, towing the Navy's coal up the river, don't signify at all compared with what you fellows done up there in Tennessee. I heard you broke Hood's entire army that day before you pulled back to Nashville. Took all the fight they had left right out of 'em that day in Franklin, I know." Removing his cap, he added, "My hat's off to you and your comrades, sir."

Then it was young George's turn to be embarrassed, "Gosh, I didn't mean that Tom and his crewmates done anything that was all that brave. I just thought it made a funny story, fooling that old devil Forrest like that." Just then the gathering tension was broken as someone rang the bell calling them to table for a hymn, a blessing and supper.

Tom craned his neck trying to locate Roxa in the crowd. When he finally saw her, his heart sank as he noticed that she was talking and laughing with some younger men, closer to her own age. When she noticed him, however, she stopped, excused herself and moved through the crowd to his side. "Tom. I'm real glad you're here. Come and join us, Tom. We're sitting over there with Brother Conyers and his family. You remember him."

"Sure I do. Don't you think he'll mind a stranger sitting with him? I'm not even a Baptist," he said, half joking.

"Course not. I never thought to ask you what church you go to, Tom. Some folks here say you're Irish and probably a Roman Catholic. Is that true? I don't think I ever met a Catholic before."

"It's true all right. My folks came over from Ireland in '42. There's lots o' Catholics in our town, and my father helped build our church. We're not supposed to go to other churches. Our priest says it's a sin. But I don't see no harm in it. We all believe in Jesus Christ, don't we?"

"Oh, Tom, of course we do. But don't Catholics believe in all sorts of other things too? And what about the Pope? People around here say you can't follow the Pope and still be a true American. Maybe Brother Conyers can help us understand."

Following Roxa past the table where the food was laid out – lots of ham, chicken and vegetables – Tom filled his plate and went with her to join her family and the pastor's at the head table. Without a hint of shyness or anxiety, Roxa started the conversation by asking Brother Conyers flat out to explain the difference between Baptists and Catholics. The pastor was already aware that Tom was almost certainly a lifetime "Papist", and, having succeeded in the past in winning a few souls away from the Roman church, he proceeded carefully, not wishing to offend Tom or belittle his faith.

Tom was fascinated by what Brother Conyers explained. It all seemed so simple and straightforward compared with the complex catechism he had been taught by the sisters at the little convent in Brownsville. Finally, Brother Conyers offered to spend some time with Tom in private to talk to him further about "receiving Jesus as his personal savior." Tom could see no harm in that, either, and said he thought it was a very kind offer indeed. He relaxed and smiled at the company around the table as he thought of spending the summer with such a friendly, hospitable community, not at all like the fearsome "black Protestants" his parents talked about at home.

After supper, Tom was not quite ready to return to his lonely cabin on the *Sam Brown*. The golden setting sun was still shining across the river from the West Virginia side, lighting the dusty Racine road along the bank below the church. And, so, he was thrilled and delighted when Roxa took his arm and asked, "Why don't you walk home with us, Tom? Mother and Albert are driving my grandparents back to their place in the buggy, but me and George are going to hoof it. Come on, we can talk along the way."

Tom needed no further encouragement. He liked George Powell a lot, seeing him as a younger version of himself when he had started his own career on the river. And the way he felt about Roxa – well, "like" did not begin to do justice to it. Although he had met her only three days earlier, he felt sure he was falling in love with her. He loved the way she spoke her mind right out, letting everyone know what she thought. Being with her made him want to be a better man somehow, to be less awkward, tongue-tied and self-conscious. But most of all it made him want to hold her tight in his arms and kiss her freckled face, dimpled cheeks and sweet lips.

As the trio started up the road together, headed for the Powell farm, Roxa did not let go of Tom's arm but rather held it tight, pressed against the side of her firm left breast. Tom walked her slowly, enjoying the tingling sensation that the warm pressure of her breast stirred within him as he pretended to listen to George, who ambled along on her other side and described to Tom the occupants of each house they passed on their way through the village. Tom wished the walk would never end.

Chapter Nine

In late September, the leaves turned color, the nights became frosty and the fall rains arrived. On October 5 the waters of the Ohio reached their lowest point and gradually began to rise again. Tom knew that, within a few weeks, the captain and crew of the *Sam Brown* would come back to Antiquity, and he would have to return to work on the river. He had spent a wonderful three months in Antiquity, and his life would never be the same. He and Roxa were in love and promised to each other forever.

The Powell family had treated him like another son, and he had worked on the farm with them all summer, getting to know and love them, too. They approved of the courtship with one condition. Tom would have to become a Baptist before the Varians and Mrs. Powell would agree to an engagement. And before he and Roxa could marry and raise children, Tom would need to have sufficient financial means to support a family on his own.

Tom was trying to sleep. But one thought – and one thought only – kept gnawing at him, keeping him tossing and turning late into the night in his tiny cabin: How would he ever explain all this to his parents? They would never accept his leaving the Catholic Church and becoming a Baptist, no matter what the reason. Never.

Well, what they didn't know wouldn't hurt them, not for a while, anyway. There was no hurry. He could wait until the engagement was announced and a wedding date was set. Maybe by then their attitude towards Protestants would soften some. If only they could meet Roxa, then they would understand why he couldn't afford to lose her. But he and Roxa would have to keep their plans a secret for now, at least from his parents. Finally he fell asleep, his body worn out from a long day of harvesting vegetables in the cold drizzle.

A voice awakened him. "Hello on board. Anyone there?" It was the young messenger boy from the telegraph office in Racine, just four miles down the river. "Got a telegram here for Tom Malone."

Tom went out on deck, yawning and stretching, and beckoned to the boy. "That's me, sonny, bring it on up here." Tom signed for the telegram and handed the boy a nickel. The message was from Captain Sam in Brown's Station, announcing the imminent arrival of the crew and instructing Tom to begin preparing the boat for travel. Tom knew that time was money as far as Brown's Line was concerned. The crew would begin drawing their pay the day they left Pittsburgh, and Captain Sam would not be happy at all if they had to wait in Antiquity before getting underway.

He decide to go back to the farm to tell the Powells he would be leaving in a few days, then get busy seeing to the boat, checking on the fuel, water and stores and getting ready for the two hundred forty mile journey back to Pittsburgh. Fortunately, there were some small, independent coal mines nearby, and Tom could top up the fuel flat and the bunkers at very low cost. He would see about getting some wagon loads of coal as soon as he broke the news of his leaving to Roxa and her family.

When Tom arrived at the farm, he found Albert and George boiling a huge vat of water over a log fire out in back of the barn. Mrs. Powell and her father had caught the pig by the ring through its nose, and they were enclosing it in a small pen beside the vat of boiling water. The pig seemed to sense what was about to happen and was squealing loudly. Roxa was nowhere to be seen.

George called out, "Hey, Tom, want to give us a hand? This pig is ready for butchering."

"Sure, I guess so, why not? I've helped my folks a couple of times, though it ain't exactly my idea of fun. Where's Roxa, anyway?"

"Said she had some items to collect down at the general store, Tom. Seemed to be in a hurry." George chuckled and poked up the fire.

Tom laughed. Good for Roxa, he thought. He was glad she had chosen not to witness the bloodletting about to occur. This was not a nice job for a young girl. Of course, he thought, after Roxa's father, Nathaniel Powell, then mate on the side-wheel packet *Crescent,* had died back in '56 of the fever on the Lower Mississippi, Roxa's mother, a young widow with three small children, had run the little farm herself until her sons were old enough to take over. She had to get used to men's work, and probably so did Roxa.

No sooner had that thought crossed his mind than Tom observed that very lady going into the house and reappearing with a twenty-two caliber rifle in her hands. She approached the pig, which had suddenly become quiet, took careful aim and put a single bullet right between its eyes. Stunned but still alive, the pig collapsed on one side, and Grandpa Varian quickly cut its throat with a sharp knife. The pig's still-beating heart pumped great gouts of blood out of its severed throat until it died and lay still.

Now the time had come for Tom to pitch in and help the others. After first washing off the blood and mud, the four men picked the two-hundred pound carcass up by the legs, laid it across two lengths of chain and lowered it into the scalding vat after carefully checking the water temperature. Too hot and the skin would start cooking, causing the hair follicles to contract and "setting" the hair in place. Using the chains to turn the carcass in the hot water, they kept it moving until the skin was soft. Then they heaved it up on a heavy wooden table and scraped off the hair, keeping the carcass wet with warm water as they worked. Finally, when all the hair had been removed, they strung the carcass up on a horizontal wood beam by its hind legs and began the butchering.

It was at this point that Tom announced the news of his impending departure for Pittsburgh. "It won't be for a few more days, but I might not be able to help out on the farm no more, 'cuz I have to get the boat ready."

The Powells were not surprised to hear Tom's news. Other men in their little river community, including themselves, were also getting ready to return to their winter jobs on the riverboats. The harvest was in and the late crops planted, and soon Antiquity would be left without a number of its men folk, those lucky enough to have a source of income from the river to tide them and their families over until the following summer.

George spoke for the others. "Thanks for helping us, Tom. You'll be missed here on the farm. Can you come back again next year when you stop moving coal downriver? You could earn your bed and board with us, and maybe we could even pay you a share of the farm's earnings if we have a good year."

Tom was touched by George's generosity. There was no place on earth he would rather spend the following summer than there on the Powell's little farm, close to Roxa. Then it came to him. Of course. He would simply tell his parents that he had found a good summer job on a farm in Ohio while taking care of the boat. He could say he had done so well that he had been invited back for next summer. No need to go into detail about wedding plans or churches. That could come later.

Tom arrived at the little general store just in time to meet Roxa, who was coming out the door carrying a marketing basket full of brown paper parcels. She greeted him with a kiss on the cheek but then recoiled, wrinkling her nose in disgust. "Phew. Have you been helping with the hog butchering? You better go wash and change your clothes."

"I'll do that, darling. But first I have to tell you the news. I got a telegram from the owner this morning. The Captain and crew are on their way down here, and we'll be leaving in a few days."

"Oh, no, Tom. So soon?"

"They don't quit mining coal in the summer. The Browns have been piling it up in their tipples and coal yards all summer, waiting fer me and my boat to get back there."

"But, Tom, when will I see you again?" Tears welled in her eyes.

"Every time we pass by Antiquity, darling, I'll get the Captain to stop fer an hour or so to pick up some provisions for the cook. We can get 'em cheaper and fresher here than up in Pittsburgh. I know this great little truck farm where I can find the very best, don't I? Get your ma to save us one of them hams. And you and me can write to each other in between. Just write to me in care of the owners, W. H. Brown and Sons, up in Brown's Station, Pittsburgh, Pennsylvania." He wanted to make sure she didn't start sending letters to his parents' home address in West Brownsville. Not yet, anyway.

"You'll come back here next summer, Tom, won't you?"

"If you'll have me, you bet I will. I'll be praying fer a long, hot summer too, darling."

"Me too, Tom honey, me too." Tears streaming down her freckled cheeks, Roxa set down her marketing basket in the middle of the muddy street and hugged Tom hard, wrapping both her arms around his neck and temporarily ignoring the foul aura of pig that still surrounded him and the passers-by outside the store.

Captain Mike, the mate Ad Sykes, deckhand John Murray and all the rest of the crew arrived in Antiquity in dribs and drabs over the following week. By late October, having watched the flood level rising on the river gauge each day, Captain Mike finally decided they could take their tow of empties upstream, just clearing the shallow rapids at Letart Falls. Tom had already laid in a good supply of coal from the local mines and, with the cook, had stocked the pantry with plenty of produce, groceries and smoked meat from Antiquity. Then, on Monday, October 24, they fired up the four big boilers on the *Sam Brown*, got up a good head of steam, and collected the empty coalboats and barges for the trip upriver to Pittsburgh.

As they passed the Powell farm, pushing the rebuilt tow, Tom, who was standing the morning watch, asked Captain Mike to blow the *Brown's* steam whistle. When the loud blast of the whistle echoed off the hill behind the little riverbank farm, Roxa came running out of the kitchen door, wiping her eyes with one hand and waving a kitchen towel with the other. She was calling out to Tom, but he could not make out what she was saying above the noise of the engines and the big paddlewheel, so he just took off his cap and waved back to her, his own tears blinding him as he did so. He was already thinking of the *Brown's* next trip downriver and wondering how soon that would be.

Chapter Ten: 1871

Tom had successfully faced his mother's inquisition during his infrequent visits to his parents' house in West Brownsville that winter, though she became very suspicious when he told her he would be spending another summer in Ohio during low water, working on a truck farm. She asked him where he would be attending Mass. Fortunately he was able to tell her that there was a Catholic church, Sacred Heart Parish, in Pomeroy, the county seat just ten miles downstream from Antiquity, less than an hour by local packet. Tom had never set foot in the church himself, but he knew a few Catholic coal miners in Antiquity who attended Mass there regularly.

In the spring, Tom decided to visit his family for the Easter holiday. He thought he could allay his mother's suspicions by attending the Easter service at St. Peter's and perhaps even receiving communion with her, though he thought he had better not go to confession. Having left the pool boat moored across the river at the Alicia coal tipple on Saturday afternoon, Tom once again trudged across the old wooden bridge to West Brownsville with a small potted Easter lily ready as a peace offering to his mother.

Tom's father was near the end of his shift in the toll booth as Tom passed by with a wave. "Glad ye could make it, son," he called. "Yer brother's already here, and he's brought a young lady with him, too."

Pete Malone's visits to his parents' home were even less frequent these days than Tom's. Pete liked to spend his free time drinking and playing cards with his ex-cavalry friends. Most of the veterans of the Beallsville Cavalry had, like Pete, gravitated toward the brighter lights of Pittsburgh after the war.

The Pennsylvania and B&O railways, both built before the war, had completely bypassed Brownsville, diverting the high-value freight and passenger traffic away from the old National Road and leaving Brownsville with only the export of coal and coke and the related riverboat and barge construction business to depend on economically.

The new wave of European immigrants coming to work in Brownsville's coal mines and coke ovens changed the character of the community markedly, and many sons and daughters of the older inhabitants had, like Pete and Tom, gone elsewhere to seek a livelihood.

Tom had met Pete often in Pittsburgh during the winter and was already acquainted with Rose Davis, Pete's new lady love. Pete had met Rose at the prestigious Joseph Horne Company in downtown Pittsburgh, where they were both employed as sales clerks. Part of Tom's reason for coming home for Easter was to help Pete introduce Rose to his parents, while avoiding the limelight as much as possible himself. He hoped their mother would focus her attention on Pete and Rose this weekend and not on him.

Tom's walk home from the bridge was a mile longer now, since his parents had moved into their new home in East Bethlehem Township, just across the West Brownsville borough line. He and Pete had bought the house for them the previous winter, Tom with his higher earnings as a watchman and Pete with a stroke of luck at the poker table. They had together laid out two hundred dollars in cash to purchase the tidy little two-story house by the river, enabling the elder Malones to live rent-free for the first time in their lives and providing a little more space for overnight visitors.

As he came in the front door, he heard female laughter from the kitchen. Rose Davis was regaling his mother and sisters with tales of life in the big city. Rose had been born and raised in the small Irish Catholic community at Brady's Bend on the Allegheny River, north of Pittsburgh, and she seemed to Tom to be a perfect fit among the women in his family. Unlike Roxa, who seemed so uninhibited compared to Irish Catholic girls her age.

His mother would probably try to introduce him to more likely prospects for marriage during the weekend. She was forever searching out young Irish Catholic girls from the Three Towns for him to meet during his infrequent visits, extolling the piety of one, the breeding qualities of another. He dreaded another repetition of the useless ritual, arousing the hopes of the young women, only to cause them further disappointment. He knew he was considered a good catch by the mothers and daughters in the Irish community, with his dark, "black Irish" looks and his prospect of promotion to mate after two more years as watchman on Brown's Line towboats.

Sure enough, there was another young woman in the kitchen. Tom entered, proffering the potted lily to his mother and planting a kiss on her cheek. As usual, she thrust him away and wiped her cheek with the back of her hand, embarrassed by his display of affection. "Ach, Tom, get along wit' ye now. This here's young Bridie O'Halloran, Tom. Ye knew her brother Dan in school."

He looked at the young woman. She must be nearly twenty now, probably going up the hill to daily Mass with her mother every morning. "Hello, Bridie. How's Dan doing?"

"Oh, he's fine, Tom. Working in Pittsburgh. But he'll be here for Easter." She flushed, lowering her gaze.

"Give him my best, will you, Bridie?" Turning to Rose and his sisters, he gave each of them a light kiss on the cheek.

"Where's Pete hiding, Rose?"

Rose looked away. She seemed troubled. "He went off to rush the growler at the hotel before yer Dad comes home, Tom. They probably met each other in the bar down there."

Jack Malone, following his disastrous bout of drinking hot whiskeys to relieve the pains of his rheumatism, had recently renewed his temperance pledge, first taken in Ireland thirty years earlier. It seemed, however, that the pledge applied to strong drink only and not to draft beer. Giving Rose a knowing look, Tom shook his head and rolled his eyes heavenward. So the two of them were off to the races again.

Tom's mother broke the silence. "Now don't ye be fretting about yer Da, Tom. He's ever so much better since he laid off the whiskey."

Bridie stood up and smoothed her dress with her hands. "I'd better be going off home, Mrs. Malone. My mother's fixing supper, and she'll need some help. Goodbye, Tom. Nice to see you."

Tom smiled at her and nodded, relieved that she was not going to be exposed any further to their family matters.

As Tom had hoped, the rest of the evening went smoothly, with Pete and Rose receiving all the attention, especially after Pete announced to the family gathering that he and Rose were planning to be married. After making sure that Rose was indeed a devout Catholic girl, Margaret Malone beamed with satisfaction and gave her a hug. "Welcome to the family, Rose dear. Have ye set the date yet?"

"No, ma'am. Pete and I will be going up to Brady's Bend in a week or two to visit my parents, and we'll be talking to them about wedding plans."

"We've an old saying back in Ireland, Rose, 'Marry in April if you can. Joy for maiden and for man.' Maybe yez can get married right after next Easter. That'd be a year from now."

With a shock Tom realized that his mother was probing, not very subtly, to see if perhaps Rose was already in the family way. He prayed she wasn't. To his relief, however, she smiled and nodded, "That's what we were thinking too, Mrs. Malone. We need some time to plan, since all our friends are in Pittsburgh and the wedding will be at St. Patrick's Church in Brady's Bend."

Margaret Malone looked amused. "Sure, and isn't St. Patrick's the little old log church built by the poor Irish settlers from Donegal who crossed the Allegheny River back in the 1790s? Why, it's even older than the old brick church that burned down here just before Jack and me arrived from Ireland in '42."

Rose flushed. "We haven't used that awful old log building for ages, Mrs. Malone," she retorted. "Why, we've had a nice brick church in Brady's Bend for years now. It's even older than I am, and everyone says it's the most beautiful church in our diocese. It'll be just perfect for our wedding."

"'Tis a fine thing to take pride in yer Parish, Rose dear, but just wait 'til ye see *our* beautiful *stone* church the morrow. My Jack helped to build it with his own two hands, so he did. He learned to work with the stone before we were married, and he used to put in a few hours on the weekends helping the stone masons our pastor brought over from Ireland after the old church burned down."

Score another one for our Mam, Tom thought with a chuckle. Right. Welcome to the Malone family, Rose dear.

Tom knew he could not avoid his mother's inquisition much longer. Having more or less approved of her elder son's choice of partner, she would now return to matchmaking for him with a vengeance, or at least demand to know the reason for his reluctance. Much as it pained him to do so, he would somehow have to keep concealing the truth about his planned marriage to Roxa from his parents.

Why not just tell them part of the truth, that he would not be able to support a wife and family until he became eligible for promotion to mate in early '73? That was truthful. He could then say that he wanted to be free to "play the field" until then, rather than becoming engaged for two years. Would she believe him? She had to.

The whole family was up early on Easter morning, climbing the long hill to St. Peter's with a crowd that included many "C and E" worshipers, people who only came to Mass twice a year on

Christmas and Easter. They would probably not line up to receive Communion for fear that the priest would turn them away at the altar, although they were probably not yet officially excommunicated.

Although Tom was well known in the Parish, he had been away on the river and in Ohio for most of the last two years. Father Heaney had moved on to another assignment, and the new pastor, an Irish priest named McHugh, had arrived while Tom was in Antiquity and barely knew him. He was determined to receive Communion from Father McHugh, however, even though he had not been to confession nor received absolution in several years. If he did not do so, his mother would immediately become suspicious, and he was not yet ready to reveal his and Roxa's secret engagement to his parents.

As Father McHugh intoned the *Agnus Dei* and elevated the Host toward heaven, Tom glanced over at his mother, who was deep into counting her Rosary beads, paying no attention to Father. He was sure she would be watching him like a hawk when the time came to receive, though, and he steeled himself for an act that – he had always been taught – was a sin. Was it really? Only God could judge. He had also been taught that it was a sin for him to attend a Protestant service, but he had never felt God's presence as intensely as he had in the little Baptist church in Antiquity.

When his turn came, he followed his parents to the altar and received the host, his mouth dry, pulse racing. On the way back to the pew, he caught his mother's eye. She was smiling at him, satisfied at last that he had not abandoned his Catholic faith. He tried to smile back at her. It had worked.

Now he would just have to plant the half-truth about not wanting to be seriously involved with a girl until he could get his promotion to mate, and he could buy the time he needed. He and Roxa could marry in two years. When it was official, he would bring her home to meet them and break the news. Surely, once they met her, they would love her as he did, and they could not possibly object to the marriage then, or could they?

Chapter Eleven

As he stood his watch in the *Brown's* wheel house headed upriver one night in early June, Tom was happy and content. A full moon lit the river with silvery light that sparkled off the little ripples ahead of them, making the river look as if it was studded with thousands of tiny lights. Tom loved the river and was thinking how much his life had been influenced by its yearly rise and fall. It had carried him far away from his parents, brought him safely through the war to a whole new life with Roxa and her family. Now, the receding water meant only one thing: soon he would be back in Antiquity for the summer.

Tom's reverie was interrupted by the arrival of Ad Sykes, the mate. It was four in the morning, the usual breakfast time on the *Brown*, and Ad was just beginning his six-hour watch, relieving Tom until after dinner at ten o'clock. "Pancakes this morning, Tom. Better go and get you some before they're all gone."

Tom needed no urging, not having eaten since his four o'clock supper time the day before. He was hungry and tired. But he had something more important on his mind, for they were nearing Point Pleasant. Tom had a deal with Captain Mike and the cook. Each time they passed Antiquity, the *Brown* would stop briefly for provisions. Tom knew the best sources of produce, meat and groceries, and the cook could get what they needed for a fraction of the prices in Pittsburgh. While he and the cook were ashore with the yawl boat, Tom would run the quarter mile down to the

Powell farm to see Roxa for a few minutes. She usually had a warm piece of pie and a cup of coffee waiting for him. He hated to tear himself away from these brief visits, but a deal was a deal, and, when the marketing was done, a short blast of the *Brown's* whistle would call him back to duty.

Roxa, wearing a pretty pinafore over her dress, was waiting for him in the kitchen when he arrived, out of breath. She had learned to recognize the distinctive sound of the *Brown's* whistle as she approached Antiquity. She hugged Tom tight and kissed him. "You look worn out, darling. Are you not well?"

"It's these night watches. Ever since I made watchman, I've been working from ten at night 'til four in the morning while the mate sleeps. I just don't get enough rest during the daytime. I can't wait 'til I get promoted, you and me can get married, and I can make some other poor fellow take the damned night watches for me."

Roxa laughed, delighted. "Shh. Don't let Mother hear you cursing."

He smiled. "Oh all right. Now fetch me my coffee, woman. I haven't got all day."

"Aye, aye, Captain Tom, sir." Roxa, still laughing, gave Tom a mock salute, sat him down at the table, placing his pie and coffee in front of him. "How soon do you think you'll be coming to stay for the summer, darling?"

"Might not be too long. Not much of a flood this year, and the river's already pretty low. Mebbe another month or so, and we'll finish the season. Brown's don't want to get her stuck down here again like we done last year."

"And then you'll come straight back to us, won't you? Oh, Tom, I miss you something awful when you're away."

Tom's prediction of an early halt to navigation proved valid, and by the Fourth of July he was back in Antiquity again, ready to become a Baptist and seasonal farm hand. After a few evening sessions with Brother Conyers, discussing the differences between Baptist and Catholic beliefs, he reaffirmed his wish to convert and responded to the next altar call in church to accept Jesus as his personal Savior. Soon afterwards, Brother Conyers and the entire congregation accompanied him down to the river for his first baptism as a "believer." Like most Catholics, Tom had been baptized as an infant, though, for some reason, his parents had waited until he was almost three years old to take him to the old stone font at St. Peter's. Brother Conyers told him, however, that his earlier baptism didn't count, that he would need to be baptized again as an adult.

Tom had no recollection of his Catholic baptism, but he had learned from the nuns in Brownsville that his godparents had promised, on his behalf, that he would renounce the devil and believe in all the affirmations of the Apostles' Creed. He could see no harm in any of that, nor in repeating the same promises for himself as an adult in a second, Baptist ceremony.

Anti-Catholic feeling ran high in America that summer. Pittsburgh newspapers arriving by packet at Apple Grove carried reports from New York City of a terrible riot, for the second year in a row, on July 12, "Orange Day", when another Irish Catholic mob had attacked the Protestant parade marching down Eighth Avenue. More than sixty people were dead this time, mostly Irishmen, and hundreds were injured as a result of the fighting.

Tom was shocked and disgusted by the news, which made him even more resolved to leave the Catholic Church. How could people all claiming to be followers of Jesus inflict such hatred and violence on one another? He knew his parents had always hated Protestants, but he himself had many Protestant friends from his school days back in Brownsville and his years on the river, and he had never really understood why his parents felt the way they did. The people of Antiquity were so kind and hospitable that he felt more at home with them than he did with his own troubled family.

The day of Tom's rebaptism dawned hot and muggy, threatening a shower. Broad expanses of river bottom had been exposed by the receding waters below Letart Falls, and the crowd of triumphant worshipers, happy to be claiming a convert from the despised Roman faith, were able to walk on dry, sandy ground as far as a pool in the shallow water just north of the church. They sang hymns as they accompanied Tom and the Powells to the ceremony. Tom was wearing a white robe, walking hand in hand with Roxa as he approached Brother Conyers, who waited for him in the waist-deep water.

The actual baptism went quickly, as Tom had already confessed his faith earlier in church that morning. Brother Conyers laid him down backwards in the still, tepid water, placed one hand firmly on his head and thrust him all the way beneath the surface. When Tom re-emerged, spluttering, Brother Conyers embraced him. "You're born again, Tom, washed clean of your sins in the blood of the Lamb. Welcome to our congregation, son." Tom actually did feel cleansed and invigorated by the muddy water, set free somehow from the personal demons that had tormented him since childhood. Whatever his parents and the Catholic Church might say or do to him from now on, he knew he would somehow be all right. He really was "born again" – and now he believed he had a direct, personal relationship with Jesus, his Savior, no longer dependent on a priest's mysterious Latin words at the altar, somehow magically delivering Jesus to him in a little bit of bread. Nobody in between now, just him and Jesus.

As the little crowd on the riverbank began singing a hymn, Tom waded through the water with Brother Conyers to the place where the Powells were standing. Roxa, her eyes shining, hugged him tight, not minding his wet robe.

Tom did not think it fitting to sleep in the Powell's farmhouse, even though he and Roxa were now officially engaged to be married in the little Baptist church as soon as he was promoted to mate in early '73. That would happen only after he spent the remainder of that summer, and the whole of the following one as well, working on the Powell farm. The decision to wait until he was promoted to mate had been partly his own, and he was

determined to stick to it. In the meantime, he did not want
tongues wagging in the village.

With Roxa's help and a saw, hammer and nails, he fixed himself
a little place to sleep in one corner of the barn. He moved
Albert's old bed and washstand out there and an old wardrobe
and dresser to store his clothes. He had left all his cold weather
gear back on the *Brown,* so he didn't need much storage space.
When the job was finished, he turned to Roxa. "We mustn't ever
meet each other out here, darling. We'll only meet outdoors or in
the house from now on. I don't want to give those old
busybodies in town anything to gossip about where we're
concerned. Agreed?"

"Oh, pshaw. I guess so, if you really insist. But I think you are
being silly to worry." She leaned her head to one side, eyeing
him with one eyebrow raised.

"It's for your own sake. A woman's most prized possession is
her reputation, and I don't want anything to happen to yours."

He could tell she was pleased by his concern for her reputation,
even though she pretended to be cross with him. A girl's
reputation, once lost, could never be recovered again. He had to
keep reminding himself of their age difference. Roxa was still
only a girl, just turned eighteen, seven years younger than he was.

As they turned to go back to the house, Roxa reached out to
stop him. "I love you, you old bear." She reached up and flung
both arms around his neck, pressing her body tight against his
and kissing him. "There. That'll give you something to
remember when you're out here all by yourself."

Tom learned many new things that summer – how to milk a
cow, how to plow a straight furrow, how to use a scythe, how to
rake and stack hay. Most importantly, he learned about love. Not
just the love between himself and Roxa, which grew deeper and
stronger each day, but also the love shared by the whole
Powell/Varian family. There was enough love to go around for
all of them and plenty more left over for him. He had never
known such love at home in Brownsville, where any public sign

of affection had been frowned upon and strict Catholic piety and fear of punishment had ruled his life.

But the days were gradually growing shorter and the nights longer and cooler, and Tom knew that the Ohio would soon stop its fall and begin to rise again, calling him back to his job on the *Brown*. Most rivermen on the Ohio led similar double lives, dividing their time between steamboating in the winter and some other occupation on land during the summer. He would have to continue living this way even after he and Roxa were married, he knew, so he had better get used to it.

He had not minded in the least leaving his parents home or his summer jobs at the boatyard or Brown's Station to go back to work on the river each fall, but he knew he would feel differently about Antiquity and his new family. A sweet sadness filled him as he thought of leaving again. He went to find Roxa. He was learning for the first time how to share his feelings, and he wanted to tell her how sad he was feeling about the rapidly approaching day of their parting.

He found Roxa in the spring house, working the butter churn, and he took over the task for a while. Easier to talk about difficult subjects with something to occupy his hands. The churn was a new one, made of brown stoneware with a picture of a chicken done in black glaze. It held four gallons of cream and had an old fashioned vertical dasher with a polished wooden handle that went up and down, up and down, churning the cream into buttermilk and butter. Tom placed his big hands on the handle next to Roxa's small ones, adding his strength to the rapid up and down motion of the dasher. They sat facing each other, their legs spread apart, with the heavy churn on the spring house floor between them.

"I need to talk to you, Roxa. I was feeling sad just now, and I had to come and find you. The river's so low now it can't get much lower. October's almost gone, and soon I'll be getting the call from the owners to go back to Pittsburgh and get the boat cleaned up and painted for the winter."

"I feel awful sad to think about you leaving, too. I've been trying not to, but with the leaves starting to fall, I can't help it."

Tiny beads of perspiration moistened Roxa's forehead, she was breathing hard, her lips were slightly parted and her cheeks were flushed from the effort of working the butter.

Tom felt himself becoming very aroused by the intimacy of their positions, knees apart, almost touching, and the steady lifting and plunging of the thick wooden handle they held between them. Could she be feeling it too?

As they sat there working the churn together, he was sure that they were both thinking of the same thing, but they mustn't allow themselves to act on those delicious thoughts until they were husband and wife.

The lump of butter hardened inside the churn, and the dasher began to bump and buck. The polished handle became slippery with the sweat from their hands. Then – was it an accident? – Tom's hands suddenly found Roxa's and grabbed them. He pulled her toward him above the churn and their lips met hungrily. Leaning forward, she pulled his hands toward her with a soft moan of desire and rubbed his palms against her firm young breasts as they continued to kiss, their tongues exploring each other.

He knew that Roxa was his for the taking at that moment if he wanted her, but he stopped just in time. Thank God for that churn standing between them. She was so innocent, surely a virgin, and only eighteen, while he was twenty-five and a man of the world. He had to be responsible.

Her grip on his hands went limp as she sensed his hesitation, and the kiss ended as suddenly as it had begun, with both of them breathing hard and out of control. "Oh, Tom, I want you so much. How will we ever survive the next eighteen months?"

The river reached its lowest point on October 11, and the next week the telegram they had been dreading arrived from Captain Mike in Pittsburgh.

"For Tom Malone c/o Powell, Antiquity, Ohio, near Racine stop report on board soonest stop expect good coalboat water by November first stop regards Dougherty"

Tom had been expecting the summons and was ready, if not very willing, to pack up and leave the farm. He had been obeying the call of the river each fall for seven years. The Powell women were river people too and well accustomed to seeing their men off to faraway places each year. But it still came as a jolt, a sudden change in the daily pattern of their lives, with empty places at the dinner table a sad reminder of absent men folk.

After a last, silent breakfast on the farm, Almira Powell and Roxa hitched the horse to the buggy and drove Tom and his bag over to Apple Grove, above the falls, to catch a ride on a local packet. The small, shallow-draft "low water boats" could keep operating from Apple Grove during most of the summer.

They had timed their arrival at the landing to coincide with the scheduled departure of one of the smaller packets. It would carry Tom only as far as Parkersburg, where he would have to change to a larger boat or a train for the rest of the journey.

Tom was glad to see that the packet was already taking on passengers and freight. He did not want to prolong the agony of their parting any more than necessary. Besides, he and Roxa had been saying goodbye to each other for days, ever since the arrival of the telegram.

"I'll write to you just as soon as I know about our next trip downriver." His throat tightened and tears welled up, blurring his sight of her.

"I'll have a nice piece of pie waiting for you." She forced a smile, then sobbed, "Please take care of yourself."

And then it was over. He was aboard, standing on the foredeck of the little steamboat with his bag, waving his cap as they backed away from the landing. The pilot made a careful turn into the shallow, narrow channel, tugged the whistle cord and headed upriver. As they rounded the first bend, Tom took a last, fond look at Roxa and her mother standing in the distance, still waving goodbye.

Chapter Twelve

Once again, Tom found himself walking through the big covered bridge over the Monongahela. It was Christmas Eve, and he was on his way to his parents' house in East Bethlehem for the long holiday weekend. He had not seen or heard from them since Easter, and he was not looking forward to spending the holiday with them. Of course, it would be nice to see his sisters again, and Pete and Rose were also coming for the holiday. But going to midnight Mass under the ever-watchful eye of his mother was a prospect he did not relish.

Tom had a bag of gifts slung over his shoulder, things he had found in the shops in Pittsburgh. Warm shawls for the girls, a new china teapot for his mam and a big box of Havana cigars for his da. Pete and he had agreed not to exchange gifts this year, since they were both rather out of pocket after buying gifts for the others. Pete's gambling had not been going well, and he was beginning to worry about how he would support Rose after they got married. Their wedding date was set for Saturday April 13, just two weeks after Easter.

Tom smelled the turkey as soon as he opened the front door, and he also detected another, all too familiar smell. As usual, everyone was crowded into the kitchen, and his father and Pete were already enjoying some advance Christmas "cheer" from the big wicker-wrapped demijohn of Old Overholt "sipping whiskey" Pete had brought his father from the distillery near Scottsdale in neighboring Westmoreland County. Someone, probably Rose, had tied a big red bow around the handle of the wicker basket to make it look more like a Christmas present. Tom's heart sank as he realized that, thanks to Pete's thoughtless gift, their father's struggle to stay away from strong drink had suffered another setback.

Setting down his bags, he made the rounds, first kissing his mother, his sisters and Rose on the cheeks and then solemnly shaking hands with his father. "Merry Christmas, Da," he murmured. He still always felt a little afraid of the old man, especially when he was drinking.

Although he knew that his straight-laced brother would not partake, Pete teased, "Come on, Tom, it's Christmas, for Heaven's sake. Have a drink with us. This is guaranteed genuine four year old Pennsylvania rye whiskey. It'll cure whatever ails you."

Tom glared at him. "If that was true, Pete, then you'd be the healthiest specimen alive. No thanks, someone's got to stay sober enough to carve that bird without making turkey hash out of it, brother, and I can see that you two won't qualify for the job."

Far from being offended by Tom's angry response, Pete and his father just roared with laughter and refilled their empty glasses. Tom glanced at his mother, whose deepening frown foretold a stormy night ahead for the whole family. Thank God he was only spending the one night with them.

Later that evening the turkey dinner, duly carved and served by Tom and his sisters, counteracted some of the effects of the whiskey. By eleven o'clock, the entire Malone family were able to make their way across the river and up the hill toward St. Peter's Church for Father McHugh's midnight Mass.

The cold night air and the long climb put both Jack and Pete into a slightly more sober, properly repentant mental state, reinforced by the angry mutterings of Margaret, who, bundled deep in her shawl, forged ten paces ahead of the rest of the group, occasionally lapsing into the Irish to find the proper words to vent her feelings.

When they arrived, St. Peter's was already crowded with merrymakers. During the long Mass, Tom sat in the crowded pew, counting his Rosary beads distractedly, his mind far away, thinking of Roxa and her family and wishing he were sitting with them at the midnight service in the little wooden church in Antiquity.

The next morning Pete and his father were curing their hangovers from the "sipping whiskey" of the night before by taking "a few hairs of the dog that bit them", much to Tom's disgust. Margaret and the girls made turkey hash and fried eggs for the family breakfast. The rest of the day was given to visiting friends, as Margaret showed off her prospective daughter-in-law to her closest cronies, having first satisfied herself that Rose was indeed a good Catholic and not yet pregnant.

Back in Pittsburgh, navigation on the upper Ohio came to a halt due to ice, and Tom was on furlough until after New Year's Day. Rose and Pete invited him to accompany them up the Allegheny to Brady's Bend to spend the holiday with Rose's parents. Pete confided that he could use Tom's moral support for the occasion.

The Davises, though relieved that someone wanted to marry their eldest daughter, already twenty-seven and well on the way to permanent spinsterhood, did not entirely approve of him as husband material, Pete explained. Anthony Davis was the assistant superintendent at the Brady's Bend Iron Works, having worked his way up the ladder from the mill floor to the front office. He had hoped for a better match for his daughter. Pete allowed that his past visits to Brady's Bend had been tense affairs, punctuated with periods of awkward silence.

This time, however, Pete said, it seemed that the Davises had finally accepted him into the family and would formally introduce him to Brady's Bend "polite society" at the usual round of New Year's Day open-houses, parties and visits, beginning with an engagement party at the Davis home on New Year's Eve.

Pete and Rose met Tom at Union Station early on Saturday morning, December 30. As they purchased their tickets, they were dismayed to learn that they would have to catch their return train from East Brady at 5:19 a.m. on Tuesday morning to be back in Pittsburgh on time for work at Joseph Horne's.

They boarded the nine o'clock Buffalo Express to make the seventy mile run up the Allegheny River, stopping at East Liberty, Oakmont, New Kensington, Kiskiminetas Junction, Kittaning and Red Bank on the way. Pete insisted on sitting in the parlor car, where he fortified himself with several large whiskeys to prepare for the weekend. Tom said nothing at the time, but the looks he and Rose exchanged spoke volumes. Arriving at the East Brady station at eleven, they hired a hackney, crossed the river on the ferry, and by noon the three travelers arrived at the Davis residence at the far end of Brady's Bend, just in time for dinner.

After introductions and a visit to the guest bedroom he would share with Pete, Tom went downstairs to join the others, finding Pete and Mr. Davis already enjoying a drink together.

"Care to join us, Tom?" Anthony Davis smiled, waving toward a large Waterford crystal whiskey decanter standing on the sideboard.

"No, thank you, sir, I don't drink." Tom noticed a Negro maid helping Mrs. Davis arrange the dishes on the dining room table. He had never been invited to a private home that employed servants before. Pete was a lucky fellow. He thought of Roxa and her mother, eking out their precarious living on the tiny farm perched on the riverbank. How he missed her.

Mrs. Davis came into the parlor wiping her hands on an immaculate apron with Irish lace trim. "Dinner is served, gentlemen. Anthony, you and Peter may bring your drinks to the table if you wish." A shadow crossed her expression as she said this. Clearly, she did not approve of drinking strong liquor at midday, even on a holiday weekend.

Their dinner consisted of roast lamb with potatoes, carrots, onions and canned vegetables on the side, one of Tom's favorites. The Davises tried to draw him into the conversation, but Pete and Rose made it difficult with their endless talk of wedding plans.

They would all be going to Mass at St. Patrick's in the morning to celebrate the Feast of the Holy Family. Rose wanted Pete to see the grand interior of the church where they would be married after Easter. "It's the most beautiful church, Pete darling. And tomorrow all the Christmas decorations and candles will still be up. Oh, I can't wait to show it to you." Rose clapped her hands with excitement and stood up. "Let's go calling on my friends this afternoon, shall we? I want to show you off, you handsome devil, you. Can Pete and I take the buggy, Dad?"

"You can if you promise to let him drive, Rosie. There's a lot of ice on the roads."

Rose gave Tom an appraising glance. "Why don't you come along too, Tom? Who knows, you might meet the girl of your dreams right here in Brady's Bend."

As they drove around Brady's Bend in the Davis' buggy, calling on all of Rose's women friends, Tom thought only of Roxa, remembering their tantalizing interlude with the butter churn. He tried to be polite and make small talk with the women, most of whom were about the same age as Rose and sadly resigning themselves to spinsterhood, but his polite smile had faded by evening, and he was grateful when Rose announced that they should return home for supper.

Pete finally succumbed to the long day's series of whiskeys, egg nogs, punches and mulled wine shortly after supper and went to bed early, snoring loudly on one side of the guest room bed. Tom had received a tender, loving letter from Roxa, addressed to him at Brown's Station, just before leaving Pittsburgh, and he took the opportunity to write a long reply to her before finally saying his prayers, blowing out the new-fangled kerosene lamp on the nightstand and going wearily to bed himself. Before closing his eyes he kissed both the letters and placed them carefully under his pillow. He hoped he would dream of Roxa.

Tom was impressed as he entered the church with Pete and the Davises the next morning. St. Patrick's Church, a brick edifice about forty-five by eighty feet, was the pride of the Irish Catholic community in Brady's Bend. Mr. Davis proudly explained that a major improvement of the church's interior had begun in 1868, and by November 1871 the work had been finished. "Just in time for Rosie's wedding," he laughed.

Tom gazed around, mentally comparing St. Patrick's with St. Peter's back home in Brownsville. The prosperity generated in Brady's Bend by the recent boom in the business of the local iron works was evident in the abundance of lavish art works, stained glass and statuary, as well as the comfortable plush cushions in the carved wooden pews. The whole effect was even further enhanced by the abundance of Christmas decorations and candles filling the church, although some of the evergreen wreaths and garlands were drying out and beginning to shed their needles.

Mr. Davis went on to explain that a newspaper reporter from Pittsburgh had visited the church just before Christmas and had written an article for the *Commercial Gazette* describing it in glowing terms and calling it "one of the finest churches in Western Pennsylvania". This had ignited a response of angry letters to the editor making sinister references to the "Catholic Menace," the recent Orange Day riots in New York City and the ongoing wave of Molly Maguire violence in the hard-coal region farther east.

Pointing to a boarded-up side window at the back of the church, Mr. Davis said that a rock had been thrown through the window one dark night the previous week, inflaming even more animosity and suspicion between the mostly Catholic community of Brady's Bend and the mostly Protestant community of neighboring East Brady, just across the river.

Tom shook his head sadly. Again he wondered how people who all claimed to follow the Lord Jesus could treat each other so hatefully.

The rest of the weekend had passed quickly. Tom had enjoyed meeting the Davis' circle of friends at their New Year's Eve engagement party that night. Gaiety, song and dance had prevailed, with a group of Irish musicians hired from the mill playing jigs, reels and polkas into the night. Both Pete, now officially introduced to Brady's Bend society, and his future father-in-law had to be helped to bed shortly after midnight. New Year's Day hangovers had been treated in the time-honored way with "hairs of the dog", and another round of return visits to their friends' "at home" receptions had followed, with even more liquid refreshments.

New Year's Night finally came, and the three visitors, quite exhausted, went to bed early, dreading the fact that they needed to be at the East Brady station by five the next morning for the trip back to Pittsburgh.

It seemed as if they had hardly closed their eyes when they suddenly awoke to loud shouts and the frightening sound of a fire bell in the street outside. Dressing hurriedly, Tom and Pete rushed up the street with Mr. Davis to help put out the fire.

When they reached the church, they could see that it was already too late; the whole building was ablaze, its elaborate stained glass windows shining out into the darkness, lit from within by the fire. The roof had already caught as the flames leaped upward from the burning Christmas decorations. The local fire brigade could only stand and watch in horror as the fire eventually consumed everything but the brick walls.

The disastrous fire, believed by most of the Parishioners to be the work of anti-Catholic incendiaries, forced the Parish to move the worship services back to their original location, the old log Church of St. Patrick, erected in 1806 using thick oak logs for the walls and split shingles for the roof. After the construction of the brick church in 1840, the old building had been used for storage, but it was still sound.

After the fire, the Davises had suggested the option of a home wedding, a tradition favored in Ireland, but Rose had insisted on having the ceremony in the old log church. She was encouraged in her wish by the new pastor, Father Herman. He was German, the first of his kind to come to Brady's Bend since 1801, when Father Heilbron had visited the area briefly to administer necessary sacraments to the little Irish frontier community.

Unable to speak English, Father Heilbron had quickly returned to Pittsburgh to be replaced by an unbroken seventy-year succession of Irish priests. The fact that the fire had occurred just a few weeks after Father Herman, their very first non-Irish pastor, had been assigned to St. Patrick's, was taken by the more superstitious souls in the Parish as a sign that their Irish Patron Saint had been seriously offended.

Led by Father Herman and Anthony Davis, the entire parish had nonetheless pitched in with a will to refurbish the beloved old log building where most of their parents had worshipped. By the time Lent began, it was ready for regular Masses, and by the arrival of Easter it had been restored to its pre-1840 charm.

Chapter Thirteen: 1872

Tom had arranged his trips down the river on the *Brown* to avoid having to spend Easter Sunday with his parents and to spend it instead with the Powells in Antiquity. The *Brown* had taken a tow down as far as Cincinnati and had returned with empties. There was still plenty of water to pass Letart Falls both ways, and Captain Mike had let Tom go ashore for the Easter weekend and had picked him up again on the way back to Pittsburgh.

The weekend on the farm had been wonderful. Spring had arrived in Antiquity in all its glory, and the Easter celebration in the little wooden church by the river had been the happiest one that Tom could remember. When it had been time to rejoin the *Brown* and his crewmates, he and Roxa had bid each other farewell once again, comforted by the realization that in only three months or so navigation would stop again, and Tom would be returning to the farm for the summer.

Now it was mid-April, and the *Brown* had just arrived back in Pittsburgh after another run downriver, this time to Louisville. Tom washed, changed into his one good suit and hurried to the landing to meet Pete, coming from work at Joseph Horne's, and their family, arriving on the steamboat from Brownsville. They would all travel together by rail up to Brady's Bend for the wedding.

Tom dreaded these family encounters. His mother always managed to turn the conversation toward his private life, questioning him over and over about his reluctance to woo any of the eligible Catholic spinsters she was always hunting down for him. He knew she suspected him of having a secret romance, but, given her hostile attitude toward Protestants, she probably never dreamed that he was already engaged to marry one.

Tom's two aunts, Katie and Eliza Malone, his father's older sisters, were also invited to Pete's wedding. They had come to America about 1840 to work as maids in the homes of two Pittsburgh businessmen and, although they were both in their early sixties, they were still employed there. Tom thought of the large family group about to assemble at Union Station for the trip to Brady's Bend. Nine people, not including Rose, who had gone ahead to help her parents make preparations for the wedding. Tom hoped their presence would distract his mother from pursuing her favorite subject.

He reached the steamboat landing just as Pete appeared in the distance, wearing the very latest in gentlemen's fashions "borrowed" from his employer's inventory. He was walking rapidly up Water Street from his job down near the Point. Good, Tom thought, let Pete take center stage when the old folks arrive. He would gladly escape being the center of their attention.

"Hello, big brother," Tom called, as Pete came within earshot, "How's the condemned man feeling today?"

"Condemned? Hardly, little brother. Actually, I'm about to move several notches up the social ladder. My prospective father-in-law didn't like the idea of having a counter jumper for a son-in-law, so he got the Iron Works to offer me a job here in their Pittsburgh office. I start right after the honeymoon. No more filling orders for ladies' unmentionables."

Tom laughed. "Wait now, wasn't it your knowledge of ladies' unmentionables that got you started on the social ladder in the first place, Mr. Lothario?"

Pete was about to respond to this gibe when a steamboat whistle echoed in the chilly morning air. The mail boat, making its first run from Brownsville, appeared around the bend, throwing out its two bow waves like a mechanical bulldog with a big white bone in its teeth. They would have to put such ribaldry aside for a while, Tom thought, and assume appropriately serious attitudes or else risk the usual angry disapproval from their mother.

When the five Brownsville Malones had disembarked on the landing stage, Tom approached his mother. He tried to kiss her on the cheek, but she pushed him away. "Ach, Tom, get along wit' ye. Not here with everyone looking on."

Once again he felt the same stab of pain he always felt at her rejections. For Margaret Malone, dour Ulsterwoman that she was, it never seemed to be the right time or place for such displays of filial affection. And yet, some childish need made him keep approaching her and being rejected.

He remembered the dark Saturday nights long ago in the little house in West Brownsville when he and Pete had shared a straw bed in the loft, listening to the sounds of their parents' furtive lovemaking from below, sounds that both frightened and fascinated him at the time. But their parents never kissed or even touched each other during the day when he was present. He wondered: Had they ever had feelings for each other anything like the ones he and Roxa had?

His father had been watching silently as this familiar family drama repeated itself once again. Tom knew his father would never react in any way to the continuing conflict between him and his mother. Besides, Da was in unfamiliar territory here in the city.

Jack Malone was obviously ill at ease now, Tom observed, standing on the landing stage and glancing around nervously at the tall buildings along the waterfront. If just being here in Pittsburgh made him so uncomfortable, Tom wondered how the old man – who had never read a book or set foot in a school – would feel about traveling on to Brady's Bend to rub elbows with "quality" folks like the Davises. He hoped poor Da wouldn't drink too much. Well, he would just have to let Mam worry about that, as he knew she would.

As the little group walked up Grant Street toward Union Station where they would meet his aunts, Tom realized that his father had probably never traveled the forty miles to Pittsburgh since first arriving in America thirty years earlier, even though his two older sisters had been living here all that time.

An hour later, Tom was looking out of the railroad car, enjoying the panorama of the Allegheny River and the hills beyond it rolling past the window, the trees putting forth their first delicate, pale green leaves of the new season. He was lost in thought, scarcely paying attention to the lively chatter of his relatives. As he had hoped, Pete was the main attraction, and his aunts, Katie and Eliza, the elderly, childless "matriarchs" of the Malone clan, took turns quizzing him about Rose and her family.

"Ach, Peter," exclaimed Katie, "ye mean to tell us they have a black couple living in their very own servants' quarters above the carriage house on their grounds?" Katie and Eliza exchanged glances, drawing down the corners of their mouths and nodding wisely to each other.

"Sure then, we'll not be telling them about our own wee garrets tucked away under the eaves of our masters' houses on Wylie Avenue." laughed Eliza.

"That we won't, Eliza dearie, ye may be sure." Katie replied, "If they ask us where we live, we'll just say we both have fine views overlooking the whole city of Pittsburgh." They both roared with laughter at their joke, their faces flushed with pleasure.

Tom turned and smiled at his aunts. Next to his three sisters and Pete, he loved the old aunts most of all. His relationship with them was so straightforward. They would never pry or try to make a match for him with some forlorn Irish Catholic spinster the way his mother always did.

"Don't you two worry none," he reassured them, "the Davises are ordinary folks like us. They just happen to have more money than we do, that's all. Why, Mr. Davis worked his way up from the mill floor to the assistant superintendent's office by hard work and good luck. That don't make him no nearer to heaven than us Malones."

At this point, Pete chimed in, "And he takes a good drop o' rye whiskey whenever he feels like it, just like me and Da."

Tom winced. Since boarding the train in Pittsburgh, Pete had been reinforcing his courage liberally from a silver hip flask whenever he thought no one would notice. Tom hoped he would not get too obviously drunk before his wedding. And Da needed no further encouragement.

The Davises had hired a large, red horse-drawn omnibus to meet the train from Pittsburgh and carry the wedding guests to the little log church up on Sugar Creek in Brady's Bend. It was licensed to carry up to twenty-five passengers, including one sitting beside the driver and twelve up on the roof when weather permitted. Someone had decorated the door and windows with bunting of white and light blue, the traditional Irish wedding colors.

The train discharged its passengers and then continued chugging off on its way north to Buffalo. The small crowd of wedding guests, recognizable by their Sunday best clothes on a Saturday morning, separated into little groups of family and friends, eyeing the people they did not know and waiting for someone to make the first move to board the bus.

Pete, unabashed as ever, spoke up in a loud, slightly slurred voice, "Howdy, folks. Seeing as I'm the lucky bridegroom let me lead the way. All aboard for Brady's Bend." He herded his family on board, followed by the rest of the guests, now laughing and chatting amiably since the social ice had been broken for them.

Their route took them across the Allegheny on a steam ferry and past the rolling mill where Anthony Davis presided on work days, crossing back and forth on little bridges over the many meanders of Sugar Creek, as the bus wound its way up the narrow valley.

They passed churches here and there, each one maintained by a different immigrant community; huge piles of iron ore, coal, coke, red dog and slag; the glowing blast furnace itself with its brick yard just behind it. Tom knew the furnace was kept burning day and night, its fire only extinguished when relining with new firebrick was needed.

Seeing the gaping white-hot mouth of the furnace made him think of what he had learned from the Baltimore Catechism as a child about the everlasting fire of hell, *"that neither gives light nor consumes what it burns, and it causes greater pain than the fire of earth..."* Would he too have to burn in hell for the "sins" he was deliberately committing day by day, each time he attended a Baptist service, received communion without absolution or lied to his parents? But how could it possibly be a "sin" to marry his sweet Roxa?

His thoughts were interrupted as Pete pointed out the local drugstore and the post office in the little town center. Then they continued on up the valley away from the smoke and noise of the iron works and coke ovens, passing the hotel on the right and the big house of the Works Superintendent on the left. Pete whispered that it was the only house in town that was bigger than the Davis's house. Finally they passed the Davis residence itself and pulled up in front of the little log church on Sugar Creek built by the original Irish settler families from County Donegal sixty-six years earlier.

As they were getting off the bus, Tom observed a gaggle of young women crowding around the front door of the church. Pete approached them smiling and asked, "Where's my beautiful bride, ladies? I hope she hasn't changed her mind."

It was supposed to be bad luck for the groom to see the bride in her wedding dress before she entered the church for the ceremony. As there was no bride's dressing room in the tiny log building, the Davises had taken Rose to Father Herman's house on the opposite side of the creek to dress there and wait until all the guests had arrived and were seated.

Finally everyone went in and found their seats. Tom was Pete's best man, standing beside him at the altar with Father Herman as they waited for Rose and her father to arrive. The interior of the church had been newly whitewashed and papered near the altar with a thin gilt paper of odd design. The Stations of the

Cross were still marked by the original rude crosses burned into the thick oak logs. Pete muttered under his breath, "Little brother, when are you going to get hitched yourself? Mam's got 'em lined up waiting for you back in Brownsville. Why don't you pick out a pretty one? Maybe one with a rich daddy like mine?"

Tom longed to share his secret with Pete, and he would have done so had Rose not arrived at that moment, escorted by her father and her best friend and matron of honor, Sue Kissane. Sue was a thin, dark-haired Pittsburgh girl who worked at Joseph Horne's with Rose and Pete. She and her husband, Joe, made a frequent foursome with Rose and Pete when they stepped out together on Saturday nights to go to dances or parties.

Suddenly the crowded room was filled with the sound of music – or rather a series of reedy wheezes punctuated by the rhythmic, but sadly off-beat, strokes of the foot pedal of a newly purchased portable harmonium – as the perspiring organist launched into a brave attempt at Wagner's *Bridal Chorus* from "Lohengrin," bringing the entire assembly scraping and rumbling to their feet on the rough puncheon floor. Anthony Davis, flushed and beaming happily, escorted his last unmarried daughter down the aisle and handed her to Pete Malone.

Later in the day, following the Mass and a champagne reception at the Davis house, Rose and Pete boarded a hired brougham under a shower of rice for the ride back to the station and the northbound train to Niagara Falls. The Pittsburgh guests followed soon after in their red omnibus to catch the southbound train back to Pittsburgh. Da had been withdrawn and silent all day, hardly tasting his first-ever glass of champagne. Thank God the Davises hadn't served any whiskey.

Tom was hoping he could sit with his aunts again on the two-hour train ride. With Pete gone off on his honeymoon, though, he was afraid he could not avoid his mother's "third degree." Sure enough, she grabbed him by the wrist as he tried to pass and pulled him down into the empty seat beside her.

"We missed ye at Easter, son. Where were ye, anyway?" She sounded suspicious.

"We had a tow for Cincinnati, Mam. I told you that, don't you remember?" Tom hated lying to her all the time, but, ever since childhood, part of him still feared her cold anger and his father's drunken rages. Just one more year. Once he and Roxa were safely married, he would bring her home to meet both of them. Then, please God, they would surely understand, and in time they would come to love Roxa too. How could they possibly not love her?

On an impulse, he reached for his mother's hand, his heart suddenly full of affection for her. Without a word, she pulled her hand away from his and turned to look out the window, frowning. His face felt hot as the blood rose. He wanted to grab his mother and shake her, to force her to accept his love, but instead he, too, turned away angrily and looked out the window across the aisle.

They sat in silence the rest of the way to Pittsburgh. Margaret Malone occasionally dabbed at her eyes with a handkerchief, but he knew her tears were not for him. He had seen her crying during the wedding too. Pete had always been the apple of her eye. Tom doubted whether she had ever cried for him, or ever would.

Chapter Fourteen: 1873

In 1871, following a rapid increase in the number of river steamboat accidents and fatalities, Congress passed new, stricter comprehensive legislation regulating inland river transport and requiring the licensing of all pilots, engineers, captains and mates. Prior to the enactment of the new law, only pilots and engineers had been licensed.

With the resumption of navigation in the fall of 1872, Tom had completed his required three years' service as a watchman. Now, however, under the new law, there was another obstacle for him to overcome before he could be promoted to mate and finally be able to marry his darling Roxa. He had to apply to the Office of the Seventh Supervising District of the Commerce Department's Steamboat Inspection Service in Pittsburgh, pass a written and oral examination and pay a five dollar fee before obtaining his mate's license.

By December 18, the river had already reached its crest and was falling. A cold snap in January clogged the Upper Ohio and its tributaries with ice, and river navigation ground to a temporary halt until the ice jam could break up. Tom seized the opportunity of the work stoppage and went early one morning to take his test at the inspection office on Water Street.

A frigid north-west wind was whipping up the ice-choked river from the Point, making pedestrians clutch their hats and mufflers as they struggled along the row of dingy offices and warehouses lining the wharf. Tom found the address he was looking for and entered, stamping the snow off his boots, grateful to be out of the punishing cold. A signboard at the foot of the stairs told him to climb to the second floor.

As he mounted the echoing staircase, Tom realized his whole future and happiness were at hazard that morning. He did not know what questions would be put to him, and he was nervous and starting to sweat in spite of the freezing weather, but he thought his experience — more than eight years on the river — would put him in good stead. Having already paid his five dollars and completed an application form by mail earlier, he entered the inspector's office through a glass-paneled door marked "Capt. Henry Dow, Inspector" in gilt letters.

Henry Dow, seated behind his large desk, was a slender, prematurely gray-haired man in his thirties with a neatly trimmed moustache and sideburns partially concealing a nasty scar that ran from his left eye to his jaw. Tom knew his reputation as one of the heroes of Vicksburg.

The inspector shook his hand and indicated a chair. Tom noticed that he wore the ribbon for his Navy Medal of Honor on the lapel of his dark blue jacket. His gunboat, the *Cincinnati,* was famous. Although hit many times by the Confederates, she kept up an attack on the Vicksburg batteries under heavy fire for hours until she was finally sunk, losing forty of her crew. Tom had heard the tale from Captain Sam himself during his days on the *Shark.*

"I see you're one of Captain Sam Brown's boys, Malone. Sam and I served together on the *Cincinnati* at Vicksburg," the inspector began, speaking with a slight Scottish burr, "I was the *Cincinnati's* boatswain's mate in those days."

"Yes, sir, I served with Captain Sam aboard the *Shark* toward the end of the war. She was my first berth as a deckhand."

"Were you on that coal run of his up the Tennessee to Decatur in the fall of '64, then? You know, the navy captured Fort Henry from the secesh way back in '62. It's a shame the army garrison abandoned it again later on. We might have kept Bedford Forrest from occupying Fort Heiman and destroying

Johnsonville if the army hadn't left Fort Henry in such an all-fired hurry."

"Yes, sir. I remember the two nights we snuck past both of them Tennessee River forts in the dark. Only one day later going back downriver and we probably would have been burned or sunk at Johnsonville with the rest."

The inspector nodded slowly, thought a while, then asked, "What lessons did you learn on that trip, Malone?"

Tom paused. He knew he must answer this question very carefully. "Sir, I learned that I would never want to run a shore battery blockade or try to climb rapids like Muscle Shoals except in a case of dire emergency in wartime. Otherwise the safety of the vessel and her crew should always come first."

The inspector nodded again, pursing his lips and touching the tips of his fingers together in front of his chin. He asked Tom a few more perfunctory questions and handed him a copy book and a list of practical questions for the written part of the examination. "I've already spoken to Captains Brown and Dougherty about you, Malone. They both support your application. If you will go into the other room and write down the answers to these questions, I'm sure there won't be any problem issuing you a license."

Tom thanked him and, already feeling relieved, went into the other room, where he found a small writing desk complete with pen and ink. After an hour of intense concentration, Tom, perspiring in spite of the cold office, turned in his copy book and question sheet to the receptionist, who told him to come back the following week for the results. Why, he wondered, did government offices always take so long to do things? Now another whole week of worrying.

A week later he returned to the Inspector's office and finally claimed his precious mate's license, number 305. He had already obtained a week's furlough from the Line, so he wasted no time making his way to Antiquity.

Roxa was with her mother, knitting beside the hot, cast iron kitchen stove, when he arrived there on a snowy afternoon. She jumped up, rushed into his arms and buried her face in his heavy woolen coat and muffler, holding him tight and not seeming to mind the damp, sheep-smelling folds of cloth, wet with melted snow.

"Oh, did you get it? Are we finally to be married?"

"Yes, darling, yes. Let's go find Brother Conyers right this minute and set the date. Let's not wait any longer than we have to. Get your warmest wrap and winter bonnet. It's awful cold out there."

The two bundled up and went out in the cold to walk down the road to the parsonage in the drifting snow. They found Brother Conyers at his supper, but when they explained the purpose of their visit, he did not mind the interruption at all. He rushed to the door to meet them, hugging Roxa and pumping Tom's hand. He, too, had been waiting for almost two years since Tom's baptism to unite the happy pair. "Hallelujah, children, praise God. Let me get my book, and we'll set a date for the wedding. Will your family need time to arrange travel, Tom?"

Tom hesitated, his face flushed. "They'll not be coming to the wedding, Brother Conyers. I hope you understand."

The happy smile vanished from the pastor's face and was replaced by a look of concern. "I'm afraid I do, Tom. They probably believe it's a sin for them even to set foot in my church. Will you be telling them at least?"

"I thought maybe I might take Roxa home to meet them during Easter weekend. They might be in a more agreeable frame of mind then." Tom felt awkward still referring to Brownsville as "home" there in Antiquity, where he truly felt much more at home than anywhere else on the planet.

As Sister Conyers cleared the supper dishes, the three sat at the table in the pastor's kitchen, also heated by a glowing cast iron stove. With a calendar and the appointment book in hand, they started to plan for the wedding.

"Mother and I will need a few weeks to make a wedding dress," Roxa said, perched on the edge of her chair, her bright blue eyes dancing with excitement. "George and Jenny will be here in town, but I need to let Albert know a few weeks ahead so he can arrange to be here too. I want him to give me away." Roxa's two older brothers lived nearby. George Powell, the younger of the two had gotten married himself the day after Christmas to Jenny Lax, nineteen years old and just off the boat from Durham, England. She had recently become the new teacher at Antiquity's one-room schoolhouse. Albert had left the river after the war and was working as an engineer at the gas and oil field east of Parkersburg in West Virginia.

Tom chimed in proudly, "Now that I finally have my mate's license, I'll be signing off the *Brown* and looking for a mate's berth as soon as I get back to Pittsburgh. That may take a while, though, so let's say a month from now for the wedding."

Roxa frowned in surprise but quickly recovered her composure and nodded wearily, "Well, if it has to be, I guess it just has to be, but I'll be counting the hours, minutes and seconds 'til then."

Brother Conyers looked at the calendar and scratched his head, "A month from now takes us to Wednesday the fifth of March. It's the second Wednesday in Lent, though, so you won't be having a big celebration, now will you?"

Roxa frowned again and sighed with disappointment. "No, I guess we won't, what with so few of our family here and Tom's folks not even coming. We'll just keep it short and sweet."

When Tom returned to Pittsburgh later that week, he discovered that Captain Sam and Captain Mike had already met to discuss his promotion to mate and were arranging a berth for him on another boat. New towboats were being commissioned to meet the steady increase in coal traffic, and deck officers familiar with the trade were in short supply. The rapidly expanding railways could not compete with the much lower rates of the towboats for moving coal.

Tom found Captain Mike and Ad Sykes drinking coffee at the dining table. "Sorry you'll be leaving us, Tom, but congratulations on your promotion. You've earned it." Captain Mike moved a vacant chair away from the table and invited Tom to sit with them.

He called to the cook, "Jeremiah, bring the Line's newest mate a cup of coffee and a doughnut."

Jeremiah, the cook, who had accompanied Tom on all their shopping excursions in Antiquity, served his coffee and doughnut with a broad grin lighting up his ebony features. "Here you are Mr. Mate, sir. Hope you enjoy the coffee."

Tom laughed, "I guess I'll have to get used to the 'Mr. Mate,' Jeremiah, but it sounds awful strange to me right now."

"Oh, you'll get used to it real quick, Tom. Don't worry." Ad Sykes reached out to shake his hand. "Congratulations and best wishes."

After finishing his coffee, Tom went to pack his gear and clear out his cabin. Then he headed across the landing with all his possessions to the Brown's Line office to find his new assignment.

Captain Sam was busy meeting visitors in his office, but he left the meeting to greet Tom in the outer office. "Good to see you, Tom. Congratulations on your promotion. I can't talk now, but you should report to Captain Leitz on the *Alice Brown* when she gets back from New Orleans in a couple of days. Captain Leitz's mate is moving up to captain, and we want you to replace him."

Tom took a deep breath. "The *Alice Brown,* Captain? Thank you, sir. Thank you." He was thrilled. The *Alice Brown,* named for Captain Sam's younger sister, was the latest addition to Brown's Line, built in Pittsburgh just two years earlier. She was big and powerful, much bigger than the *Sam Brown,* with six boilers, twenty-six-inch cylinders and a nine-foot stroke, mounted on a hull thirty-four feet wide and almost two hundred feet long, but drawing only four feet of water. She was specially designed for the long run New Orleans coal trade and usually ran there and back about every month during the coalboating season. She would usually stay below the Falls of the Ohio at Louisville, though, picking up huge fleets of coalboats and barges brought there by smaller boats and pushing them on downriver after they were reassembled below the Falls.

Tom could not believe his good luck. He shook Captain Sam's hand, turned and walked out of the office into the pale winter sunshine in a happy daze.

Tom wandered for more than an hour, daydreaming of his new post on the *Alice Brown,* before coming back to his senses and realizing that he had walked nearly five miles along Second Avenue toward the Point and was already nearing Pete's new downtown office.

He was bursting to tell his brother all his happy news. He had almost told Pete about his love for Roxa, the engagement and their wedding plans when they had met the year before for Pete's wedding. He would not ask Pete to be his best man at a Baptist wedding, though. That would involve his big brother in an occasion of sin, according to the strict teaching of the Roman Catholic Church, which did not even consider marriages in Protestant churches as valid.

But he could not keep his secret from his family any longer. He would ask Pete to keep the news to himself until Easter, when he would bring Roxa to Brownsville and introduce her to his whole family. They would surely be charmed by her, just as he had been, and then they would surely accept her lovingly into the family, wouldn't they?

Captain John A. Leitz was the first master of the *Alice Brown,* having been in command for eighteen months since her launching in September, '71. Tom found him in the Brown's Line office late in the day on Friday, February 21, just returned from another run to New Orleans. Saluting smartly, he said, "Tom Malone, reporting for duty, Captain."

"No need for formality, Tom. Good to meet you, and congratulations on your promotion. What's this I hear about you getting married next month? Is that true?"

"Yes sir, Captain Leitz. Can you spare me for a while? I'd like to start working on the *Alice Brown* right after Easter if I could."

"I guess we can work something out with the man you're replacing. He just found out when we arrived from New Orleans that the towboat he was supposed to take command of, the little old *V. F. Wilson,* was accidentally hit and sunk by a runaway loaded coalboat during the high water on Monday, right in the center of Pittsburgh harbor, just below the Smithfield Street Bridge."

"Did anyone get hurt, Captain?" Tom tried not to smile at this stroke of good luck for his wedding plans.

"No, thank God. The officers and crew were on shore at the time. Funny thing is, Tom, the *Wilson* was chartered by the government all during the war. She was Grant's dispatch boat at Vicksburg, came through that whole fight without a scratch, even brought the news of Vicksburg's capture back up north, and now she gets sunk by a goddamn stray coalboat while she's lying tethered at the wharf. Can you beat that?"

Chapter Fifteen

March began with heavy, wind-driven spring rains in Southeastern Ohio, finally breaking the drought that had plagued farmers the year before. Tom had hoped for a sunny day for the wedding, but the weather had not cooperated.

For the sake of propriety, he was still sleeping in his little nook in the Powells' barn, but after the wedding he and Roxa would finally share her bedroom in the house. Awakened by the roosters' crowing, he lay under the covers half asleep, thinking about their wedding night, hoping he would be a good enough lover in spite of his inexperience, and listening to the rumble of the rain on the tin roof.

It was gloomy outside the little window above his bed, and he felt for his pocket watch on the nightstand. In the half-light from the rain-streaked window he saw that it was already past eight o'clock. Damn. The roosters must have been fooled by the dark, cloudy weather.

He dressed quickly in his dungarees and slicker and went outside to urinate behind the barn. The cows looked accusingly at him as he passed, their udders heavy with the night's accumulation of milk.

He had a lot to do before he could even think about preparing for the afternoon wedding. He wanted to leave Mother Powell's little farm in apple pie order during their week-long wedding trip to Cincinnati, but first he must milk those cows. It hurt to urinate with his usual hard morning erection intensified by his thoughts of the wedding night. Just a little bit longer, he thought. The waiting was almost over.

His breakfast was still keeping warm beside the stove when, his morning chores done, he finally entered the kitchen after shaking the water off his boots and slicker. He poured a mug of strong black coffee, took his plate of pancakes with maple syrup, bacon and eggs and went into the dining room, where he found Roxa and her mother putting the finishing touches on the wedding dress.

Roxa did not believe in all the common wedding superstitions, and had said that, with him living right there on the farm, the idea of him not seeing her on their wedding day until they met in church was just plain silly. He loved her down-to-earth practicality.

"Morning, Tom," Roxa greeted him and jumped up from the table to give him a hug and a kiss on his damp beard.

"Morning, Roxa. How's that pretty dress? Almost ready?" He set his breakfast and coffee mug on a free corner of the table and pulled up a chair.

"Judge for yourself," she chided, holding the dress up in front of her. She looked radiant, smiling happily at him over the frilly bodice of the white satin dress. Her blue eyes danced with pleasure, and, perhaps sensing Tom's increasingly carnal thoughts, she blushed beneath the pale remainder of last summer's freckles.

"Why it's downright beautiful, just like the girl who's going to wear it."

Tom was impressed by the dress. His sister Mary, who made her living as a dressmaker, would have been proud of such a dress. He imagined himself in the privacy of Roxa's bedroom undoing, one by one the long row of little buttons that would open the center of the bodice between Roxa's full breasts when they came back to the farm that evening to spend their wedding night. He quickly sat down at the table, not wanting to reveal the swelling effect of his daydream to the two women.

That afternoon, in spite of the torrential rain, the little Antiquity Baptist Church was full to capacity with friends, relatives and well-wishers. It was the moment they had all awaited for more than two years. Albert led Roxa slowly down the aisle to where Tom and Bother Conyers were waiting. He took Roxa's right hand and placed it in Tom's left. He could feel her hand, hot, moist and trembling as she smiled up at him under her veil. His own body responded to her excitement, and his knees trembled in the trousers of his new blue serge suit.

"Will you, Tom, have Roxa to be your wife? Will you love her, comfort and keep her, and, forsaking all others, remain true to her as long as you both shall live?" Brother Conyers spoke the words slowly, his deep voice echoing above the rumble of the heavy rain on the metal church roof.

"I will."

"Will you, Roxa, have Tom to be your husband? Will you love him, comfort and keep him, and, forsaking all others, remain true to him as long as you both shall live?"

"I will."

Then the two repeated the rest of their vows, following Brother Conyers' prompting. Finally, his fingers still trembling, Tom placed a plain gold band on the third finger of Roxa's left hand, which she raised daintily to help him in his awkwardness.

"With this ring I thee wed, and with all my worldly goods I thee endow. In sickness and in health, in poverty or in wealth, 'til death do us part."

Finally, Brother Conyers pronounced them husband and wife, adding to Tom, "You may kiss the bride." But Roxa didn't wait for Tom to act. She flung both arms tight around his neck and stood on her tiptoes to kiss him, pressing herself hard against his chest. He in turn wrapped his arms around her waist and swung her right off her feet as they continued kissing.

Loud applause and laughter erupted from the congregation, who knew very well how long the two had waited to wed. Then, suddenly, it was over, and they were running out of the church under a shower of raindrops and rice and boarding a hired fringe-top Surrey, the very latest in stylish driving, with the rest of the family for the ride back to the farm and a hot supper.

After the supper dishes had been washed and put away, Mother Powell announced, "Well, it's been a long day and I'm ready for bed." She made the rounds, giving each of her children and the two new additions to her family a good-night kiss, then went off to her room.

Taking his mother's cue, Albert stood up, yawned and stretched. "Well, I guess I'll turn in too. See you folks early in the morning. Tom, I'll drop you and Roxa off at the landing on my way back to Parkersburg." He donned his slicker and headed out to Tom's little sleeping nook in the barn, where he planned to spend the night.

As he went out the door, he gave his younger brother a wink, raising one eyebrow. "George, you and Jenny must be tired too. And doesn't Jenny have to teach school tomorrow?"

"Uh, right, Albert. Come on, Jenny, let's go home and leave these lovebirds be." They, too, stood and put on their wraps for the walk to their little cottage next door.

Finally alone, Tom and Roxa exchanged wordless glances, both of them flushed and excited. Roxa took the lighted lamp from the table and with her free hand led Tom upstairs to her bedroom.

Once they were inside and behind a closed door, she put the lamp on the nightstand, turned to Tom and said, "Darling, could you help me with all these buttons?" He wondered if she had been reading his thoughts as the two began to undress each other with eager, trembling hands. Then they crawled between the chilly covers under the big feather bed. Tom was thrilled as Roxa held him tight against her firm breasts and wrapped both her legs around his, whispering, "Ooh, it's so cold. Make me warm, Tom, make me warm." And he did.

The roosters greeted another rainy day, waking Tom from a short sleep. Roxa snuggled naked in his arms in the warm bed, her head resting on his shoulder. She stirred and stretched lazily, seeking his mouth with hers for more kisses. "Get up, darling, we've got to get ready," she said.

They got out of bed and dressed quickly in the cold room, putting on their best clothes for the trip downriver to Cincinnati. Roxa stripped the bed and took the bottom sheet, spotted with her blood, to wash it. "There's only a little blood, Tom. When you were in me, so big and hard, I thought there would be a lot." Tom loved the matter-of-fact way his farm-bred wife dealt with bodily things. What a difference from his prudish Catholic family.

When they got downstairs with their bags, the whole family was waiting in the kitchen to see them off, big smiles on their faces. "Did you two sleep well?" George asked, with a knowing leer. He and Jenny were newly married themselves.

Mother Powell scolded, "Now, George, that's enough of that. It's none of your business," and, turning to Tom and Roxa, "The pancakes are ready, dears. Are you hungry?"

"I'm starving, Mother, and I'll bet Tom is too." Roxa gave George a wink and a nod, and both of them dissolved in laughter. Tom blushed in embarrassment, still not quite used to the frank, earthy banter of his farm-bred in-laws.

After a breakfast of home-made pork sausage, coffee and a short stack of pancakes each, dripping with butter and maple syrup, the honeymooners climbed aboard Albert's rig and headed for the Racine landing to catch their Cincinnati steamboat.

The stern-wheel packet *Messenger* had originally been built at the end of the war for the Pittsburgh-St. Louis trade and was now making regular trips all the way to New Orleans and back. Tom had helped to build her that summer of '65 while he was still working summers at the Brownsville boatyard while waiting for navigation to resume.

As she came around the bend toward the Racine landing, he remembered her well. Small but graceful, her hurricane deck and promenade topped by a small "texas" and crowned with a pilot house, all decorated in gleaming white paint, she reminded Tom of pictures he had seen of a fancy wedding cake. He turned to Roxa and joked, "There's our floating wedding cake, honey."

A daughter, sister and now wife of riverboat men, she knew a lot about steam packets. Her own father had died of fever aboard one of them when she was only three years old, and most folks along the river knew at least one person who had perished in one of the frequent boiler explosions. She scoffed, "Let's hope that pretty cake doesn't blow up in our faces, Tom."

They said goodbye to Albert as the pilot nudged the *Messenger* into the landing and came to a stop. After passengers and freight were discharged, the signal was given to board, and they climbed the stairs to find their stateroom, booked by Tom before leaving Pittsburgh the week before.

While Roxa was busy unpacking their things for the overnight trip to Cincinnati, Tom, brand new mate and bridegroom, went to find the captain and introduce himself. For many years he had heard of Captain Robert Greenlee, one of the oldest steamboat men in the country, who had worked on the river for forty years or more. Captain Greenlee had owned a flourishing tugboat business in New Orleans before the war but had distinguished himself, in Tom's eyes, by offering his services to the Union at the outbreak of hostilities.

Tom found the old man up in the pilot house. "I'm Tom Malone, sir. Mate with Brown's Line and just got married to Nathaniel Powell's daughter Roxa in Antiquity yesterday. We're heading for Cincy on our wedding trip. I'm honored to meet you at last, Captain. I've heard about you ever since I was a little kid."

Captain Greenlee cracked a smile and extended his gnarled right hand. "Welcome aboard, son. Newlyweds, are you? Well, please bring your lovely bride and join me at dinner. I met her dad in New Orleans before the war. Shame he died so young. A promising steamboat man he was – a mate, like you."

Dinner was an elaborate affair, five courses running from soup to nuts, including a fish course, roast steamboat round of beef over mashed potatoes and an elaborate gelatin mold, served by skilled Negro stewards in starched white coats at a large table in the main cabin. Tom had traveled some on small local packets, but he had never been on a Pittsburgh-New Orleans packet before, and neither had Roxa. The food was delicious and plentiful, and wine flowed freely, though Tom and Roxa did not indulge. During dinner, Captain Greenlee kept his young guests and a few other privileged passengers entertained with stories of New Orleans and the pre-war days on the river.

He was particularly courteous to Roxa and kept her involved in the table conversation, asking her about her family and their own experiences on the river. "You know, I met your father on his first trip downriver to New Orleans, Roxa, in August of '56. He was then mate on the towboat *Henry A. Jones* with barges full of farm produce from up here in the Great Bend Country. My tugs took charge of those barges and delivered them where they were needed. I remember your dad as a very likeable young man. A few months later, I was reading the New Orleans *Picayune,* and I was terribly shocked to find the story about his death aboard the packet *Crescent.* A sad, sad business. Only twenty-nine years old and so full of promise."

Roxa wiped tears from her eyes with her linen napkin. "I thank you, sir, for remembering him so kindly. I was just a toddler at the time, and I can hardly remember him at all. My brother Albert was devoted to him, though, and visited his grave in Natchez after the war. We still keep all of his personal effects in a trunk in the attic. I know he loved the river, just as my husband does. They both signed on as deckhands as soon as they reached eighteen. We women are jealous of that love our men have for the river. It keeps taking them away from us."

After breakfast the next morning, Tom and Roxa went out on the starboard promenade to watch the arrival of the *Messenger* at Strader's Wharf in Cincinnati. Up ahead they could see the famous suspension bridge, the longest one in the world, stretching across the Ohio to Covington, Kentucky. The bridge's two brownstone towers lifted its deck a hundred feet above the river. It had been officially opened on New Year's Day in 1867.

Tom had told Roxa about the bridge many times, but no description could come close to the impression of actually seeing it, and she squeezed his arm and whispered, "Oh, Tom, it's wonderful."

That was just the beginning of Roxa's first visit to a real city. Later that day, after checking in at a downtown hotel, they walked to Fountain Square and saw the beautiful bronze fountain, topped by a nine-foot statue of a woman with water spraying from hundreds of tiny holes in her fingertips. Then they boarded a horse car and rode out Main Street to the brand new Mount Auburn Incline, a funicular railway that lifted its passengers 312 vertical feet to the top of the hill, where they had the view of the city lights, stretching out before them all the way back to the river, as they ate their supper on the glass-enclosed veranda of the Lookout House Resort.

When they finally returned to their hotel that evening, Roxa was breathless. As they prepared to go to bed, she reached up to kiss him. "Thank you for bringing me here, darling. I never dreamed Cincinnati was so grand."

"I knew you would love it, honey." He took her in his arms and laid her gently across the bed.

Chapter Sixteen

The little steamboat huffed and puffed its way up the Monongahela from Pittsburgh. The closer it got to Brownsville, the more apprehensive Tom became. He could see that Roxa was uneasy too. Even in the best of circumstances, visiting a spouse's parents for the very first time after a secret wedding would be terrifying. But visiting *his* bigoted Catholic parents after a secret *Baptist* wedding....

They had discussed the possibility of not coming for the visit at all — of just continuing to keep their marriage a secret — but neither of them really liked that idea. Better to "speak the truth and shame the devil," Roxa had said. Besides, maybe his parents would accept the situation, since they could no longer change it. "Let's give them a chance," she had urged.   He thought she was really much braver than he was. But then she didn't know his parents. In any case, it was too late to back down now. He had written to them, saying that he was coming home for Easter, that he had a surprise for them. He felt sure they would guess the surprise was a fiancée or even a wife. They might even suspect she was a Protestant, but he doubted they would ever guess that he had converted and become a Protestant himself.

"It's just around the next bend, darling. We'll walk across the covered bridge from the wharf and hike upriver to their house. It's only about a mile." He stood and gathered their bags and the little Easter presents he had bought in Pittsburgh. "Let's go down to the foredeck and get ready to go ashore. The boat will only stop for a minute or two."

Roxa, small but surprisingly strong for a woman, took her own bag from his hand, saying, "You've got enough of a burden to carry, Tom, without me adding to it." Then she realized the double meaning of what she had just said, and they both laughed, happy to dispel the tension, as they descended the stairs and went forward to disembark.

As they began walking, Tom was pointing out the sights of the Three Towns. "That's the old wooden bridge where Da still works as a tollkeeper. It's over six hundred feet, but only half as long as the bridge we saw in Cincinnati."

"What's that big house at the top of the hill – the one with the tower?"

"We call it Nemacolin Castle, but it's not really a castle, just the house of Mr. Bowman, the richest man in town."

"It's beautiful, so many bricks."

Tom thought for a minute, then realized: there wasn't a single brick building in Antiquity.

Their footsteps echoed off the heavy planks as they walked through the covered bridge. "It's like walking through a long tunnel. But over the river, not under it," she said.

Tom laughed, forgetting for the moment what might lie in wait for them on the other side.

As they entered the little house, Tom called, "We're here. Anybody home?" There was an instant commotion from the rear of the house as his two younger sisters ran to meet them. Kate and Ellen were almost the same age as Roxa, and when they saw her, they approached her eagerly, each taking one of her arms and both talking to her at the same time. "You must be Tom's girl."... "What a smart outfit you're wearing."... "You must be tired from your trip."... "Ooh. We were sure Tom had a sweetheart, but we had no idea she was as pretty as you."...

Tom said, "This is my *wife,* girls. Roxa and I were married a month ago in Ohio. Now calm down and let her get her breath, will you?"

The two Malone sisters gasped in astonishment at this unexpected news. They let go of Roxa's arms, suddenly shy, and turned to their big brother with hugs and kisses. Ellen, recently turned twenty-one and the more adult of the two, fretted, "You've just missed Mam, Da and Mary. They've gone up to confession at St. Peter's. Oh, Tom, what will they think of you going off and getting married without telling them? And Pete and Rose won't be coming this year. They've gone to Brady's Bend for the holiday."

"I know, we met them in Pittsburgh yesterday on the way up here. And don't worry about Mam and Da. They'll be fine once they meet Roxa. Now, tell me, have you two already made your confessions, then?"

Kate, almost seventeen, said, "We have, Tom. We went early and came back so you wouldn't find the house empty. Besides, we weren't long confessing. We haven't got that much to confess." She sighed and made a sad face. "What about you and Roxie? Have you been to confession already?"

Tom hesitated, then told them a calculated half-truth. "It's 'Roxa' and, no, we haven't. It's probably too late now, so I guess we won't be able to receive communion tomorrow." He would wait until his mother's usual inquisition before telling them all the whole truth.

Tom was relieved that Roxa got to know the girls before having to face his parents. They both welcomed her into the family, asking her if she would care to accompany them back to the kitchen and help with the supper. Delighted to be asked, she went off, leaving Tom to take their bags up to the spare room, usually kept ready for weekend visits by Pete and Rose. He imagined himself and Roxa sleeping together in the double bed that night, just across the hall from his parents. He wondered how that would feel.

Tom heard his mother and older sister coming through the front door, carrying baskets of groceries. He rushed downstairs to reach the kitchen ahead of them. "Mam, Mary, this is Roxa, my wife. We were married in Ohio about a month ago."

For a moment, there was stunned silence. Then Margaret Malone turned to the younger girls. "Give us a hand with these groceries, girls." Once the baskets had been handed over, she turned back to Roxa, who had come to stand beside Tom and had taken his arm. "How do ye do, Miss…?" She paused, fighting hard to compose herself, her face flushed, her mouth working and tears of hurt and anger filling her eyes. "Arragh, Tom. Why didn't ye tell us, for pity's sake? Why did ye keep it a secret? Don't ye know we've waited and prayed for you to find yerself a wife?"

Then it was Tom's turn to be at a loss for words, but Roxa quickly came to his rescue. "It was really *my* idea, Mrs. Malone. I was afraid if you found out about me before Tom married me, you might persuade him to choose someone else – a city girl here in Brownsville or in Pittsburgh maybe. I love your son with all my heart, and I wanted to hear his vows and have his ring on my finger before I met you."

Margaret softened a bit, sighed and wiped her eyes. "Well, Tom, I still think it was wrong to keep us in the dark. But let's get supper on the table. Yer father will be coming home later, but we won't be waiting our supper fer him on a Saturday night. He'll probably just eat a pickled egg and a pig's foot at the tavern." She muttered angrily under her breath in Irish, which no one understood.

Tom had already prepared Roxa for her first meeting with his father, so she showed no surprise at this news. His mother was regarding Roxa closely, biding her time before asking all the prying personal questions Tom knew she was dying to ask. Fortunately, Margaret Malone's Ulster upbringing still made her a little diffident when meeting strangers, so Tom hoped she wouldn't start the "third degree" until the following day. Maybe by then Roxa might be able to exert her considerable charm to the extent that her religion (and his) might no longer be an issue. But, alas, he thought, that would be too good to be true.

As usual, the Malones sat down to a silent meal, another Ulster tradition. After washing up and putting away the supper dishes, they were starting to prepare for a family Rosary – to Tom's dismay – when Jack Malone burst through the door, singing Irish partisan ballads and colliding with the furniture. When Tom introduced Roxa, his father swept off his cap, bowed dramatically, took her hand and kissed it. "Ver' pleased t'meet ye, M'dear." he gargled, suddenly unable to stand and slumping into a nearby chair.

In the confusion of the moment, the family Rosary was temporarily forgotten, as Tom, Mary and their Mother half-carried Jack Malone up the narrow stairs to his bed. When Tom came back downstairs, leaving his mother and Mary to minister to the fallen warrior, he took out his pocket watch. "Well, girls, Roxa and I have had a long hard couple of days coming here from Ohio, and we want to go to the sunrise service. We'd best be getting some rest." Tom realized, too late, that he had used a Baptist expression in referring to "service" rather than "mass," but the girls apparently hadn't noticed it. They both embraced Roxa, bidding her and Tom goodnight.

Tom and Roxa left the house at five o'clock to cross the bridge and climb the long hill to St. Peter's for the six o'clock Easter sunrise service. Tom wanted Roxa to see the beautiful stone church his father had helped to build without having the whole Parish notice that they were not receiving communion.

A full moon was just setting behind Indian Hill across the river as they arrived at the church, its waning light still touching the neo-Gothic façade with pale yellow. Behind the church the eastern sky was barely aglow, silhouetting the tall steeple. "Look up there on the hill behind the church, Roxa." Tom pointed to a small log cabin. "Mam and Da lived in that little cabin thirty years ago when they came here from Ireland."

Turning back to look down at the Three Towns spread out in darkness on the banks of the river far below them, Roxa exclaimed, "What a wonderful view they must have had. It reminds me of Cincinnati." She squeezed Tom's arm against her breast and snuggled close to him.

Only a few people showed up for the sunrise service, most preferring to wait for the regular masses later in the morning to complete their Easter Duty. Tom and Roxa sat quietly at the back during the mass. Then, after hearing the priest finally intone, *"Ite, missa est,"* they went out the little side door into the churchyard, avoiding the priest and the other worshippers.

Roxa was mystified. "What was the priest saying? I couldn't understand a single word he said."

Tom laughed. "To tell you the truth, neither could I. I do know the name of the language he was speaking, though. It was Latin. But what it all meant, I have no idea."

"Do you think God understands Latin? Why couldn't the priest just talk to Him in English like everyone else does?"

Tom knew there would be nothing to eat until the rest of the family had returned home from mass, so he took Roxa for a good Sunday breakfast of fried eggs, ham, potatoes and coffee in the dining room of the big hotel at the top of Market Street. Afterwards, they continued their walk down Front Street, across the covered bridge and along the bank of the Monongahela to East Bethlehem. Returning to the house, Tom called out, "We're back. Happy Easter, everybody."

Margaret Malone was in the hall with her three daughters, putting on her best shawl for mass. "Ach, Tom, ye should have waited so we could all go to mass together. Good morning, the both o' yez, and Happy Easter. Tom, yer father is feeling out o' sorts, which is not surprising. He says he'll not be going to mass with the rest of us. I've just now taken him up a nice cup o' tea and a soft-boiled egg." She shook her head in disgust and clucked her tongue, muttering to herself in Irish.

Roxa whispered to Tom, "Is your mother speaking Latin too?"

Tom said, "Mam, Roxa thinks you're speaking Latin."

This idea tickled Margaret Malone, and, genuinely charmed for the first time, she beamed at Roxa, laughed heartily and gave her a hug. "Ah, no. T'was just a wee bit o' the Irish, Roxa dear. And I won't be repeating t'ye what it meant either."

As soon as his mother and sisters left, Tom began to relax. He was amazed at her friendly response to Roxa, quite the opposite of what he had feared. Maybe things would work out after all, he thought. If only she wouldn't start asking Roxa a lot of questions about church. He knew that, if she did, Roxa would just tell her the truth, for she never lied to anyone about anything.

It was two o'clock before dinner was ready: a fat leg of lamb with roasted potatoes, carrots and onions. As they blessed themselves and the meal, Tom saw his mother watching Roxa, who did not cross herself like the others at the table. They all tucked right in, as usual not conversing beyond the minimum necessary to have the salt passed or the tea poured. Then, while Tom and his father went outside to smoke their pipes, the five women cleared the table and washed the dishes.

Suddenly there was loud screaming and a crash of breaking crockery from the kitchen, and Roxa came running out of the house weeping, followed by red faced Mary. "Da, Mam wants you in the kitchen. Right now."

Jack Malone, still looking hung over from the night before, obediently followed his eldest daughter back into the house, as Roxa clung to Tom, her body shaking. "Oh, Tom, she found out all about us. Your conversion and rebaptism and everything. She screamed horrible words at me, words I couldn't understand. But I know she just hates me. She says she wants both of us to leave here right away, this very minute."

Tom took Roxa back into the house, his arm around her shoulder. At the door into the kitchen he met his father. "Ye damned fool. What the hell were ye thinking? Marrying a damned Protestant, and a Baptist at that. The both of yez will burn in hell fer this. Ye broke yer poor mother's heart. Don't ye ever come back here again, d'ye hear me?"

Tom tried to push past him, but found the way blocked by Mary. "Mam will not see you, Tom."

Roxa pulled back on Tom's arm and wailed, "Come on, Tom, please, let's just fetch our things and go. There's no use talking to them."

Tom felt a white-hot knot of pain rising in his throat and numbness in his hands as his own tears began to flow. She would not even see him. He was being banished from the house he and Pete had saved their hard-earned money to buy for them. He was sorry he had brought Roxa to meet them, to have her insulted and humiliated like this. What an awful mistake he had made. Of course, they had to leave. Roxa was right, staying any longer would only make things worse.

They went upstairs and collected their belongings. Then, without speaking to anyone, they left the house and began walking back into town to catch the next packet to Pittsburgh and on to Antiquity ... and *home*.

Chapter Seventeen

Tom had taken Roxa back to the farm and left her there with her family after the confrontation with his parents on Easter Sunday. She had tried hard to cheer him up on their journey back to Ohio, but he was inconsolable. The fact that Mary had sided with the old folks was an especially bitter pill for him to swallow. Mary had always been his protector when, as a child, he had been picked on by Pete. At least Pete and the younger girls hadn't turned against him. He still had half a family.

He was thinking these self-pitying thoughts, missing Roxa and feeling very lonely as he arrived back in Pittsburgh and went to the Brown's Line office to report for duty. He was just in time to join the crew of the *Alice Brown* as she was down in the harbor below the Smithfield Street Bridge, getting up steam for a trip downriver to New Orleans. After he had found his cabin and stowed his gear, Captain Leitz introduced him to his fellow officers. "Gents, this here is Tom Malone from Brownsville, our brand new mate, transferred over from the *Sam Brown*. Treat him gently now, boys. He just got married last month."

Tom made the rounds of introductions, shaking hands with each of his fellow officers. He could see that he was the youngest by ten years or so, except for the watchman, and he felt honored to be one of them. He wondered if he would even be there had it not been for his friendship with Captain Sam, a legacy from their time together on the *Shark* and their narrow scrapes on the Tennessee River in '64. But he knew damn well that he had earned his mate's license, and he would do his level best to prove to these men that he belonged here with them.

"Welcome aboard, Tom." The senior most of the group, Pilot Bill Snodgrass, a grizzled veteran of the New Orleans trade, spoke for the rest. He said that he and Captain Leitz had been with the *Alice Brown* ever since she came out of the yard two years earlier. "You won't find a better berth anywhere on the river, laddie. Captain Ike Hammitt, Jr. designed and built her right here in Pittsburgh. She's got steel outrakers and bulkheads all around — she's as safe as a house, maybe safer." Tom was grateful to know that he was now serving on the pride of Brown's fleet.

Tom knew there would be very little stopping off in Antiquity for quick visits with Roxa on the *Alice Brown*. The run to New Orleans was a little over two thousand river miles each way and usually took a couple of weeks to accomplish without stops in between. Most of the time, however, they would stay downriver below the Falls of the Ohio, rather than returning to Pittsburgh. He would be living aboard almost all of the navigation season.

He missed Roxa already, just thinking about it. Their lovemaking had been frequent, almost daily, as if they were making up for the two long years of waiting. Roxa, in bed, belied the prim and proper Baptist farm girl image she displayed to strangers. He had sensed the fire within her the very first time they had met three summers earlier—something in the boldness of her eyes and the way she had held tightly to his arm walking home from that first church supper. And yet, they both shared a firm faith in God and had been reading the Bible together each day during summers on the farm.

Tom loved reading the Bible. It had opened up a whole world of interesting characters and events of which he had had only a vague notion as a child, being taught from the Baltimore Catechism by the nuns in Brownsville. Unlike Roxa's church, his own had actually discouraged the reading of the Bible. But Tom had been given a Catholic bible by Father Heaney on his twenty-first as he was leaving home to return to the river, and he had been reading it daily ever since.

Compared with Tom's two previous boats, the *Alice Brown* was much more roomy and comfortable, with plenty of covered open deck space both fore and aft for her crew of eighteen to enjoy fresh air while off duty. A low, narrow "texas deck" stood thirty inches above the roof of the hurricane deck, lined with transom windows to provide daylight to the central passageway between the cabins. She even carried a chicken coop on the rear of her hurricane deck to produce fresh eggs and meat for the cookhouse.

Between her shiny black smokestacks hung a large sheet metal anchor tilted diagonally to starboard and painted gold, the symbol of Brown's Line. Her name, *"Alice Brown"*, stood out proudly in four-foot black and red letters on both gleaming white engine room bulkheads, while another name-plate, showing her name and home port, "Pittsburgh, Pa.", in raised white letters on a black background, was attached on the stern above her big red paddlewheel. Other sign-boards on both sides of her pilot house further identified her as part of "Brown's Line" in large black letters.

As she headed downriver from the Pittsburgh harbor for New Orleans later that day, the *Alice Brown's* "knees" were planted firmly in the middle of a large tow of loaded coalboats and barges. Tom felt a thrill of pride as he thought how powerful she must appear to the noontime crowds of people watching and waving to them from the wharf below Water Street as she passed by on her way to the Point. He hoped that Pete and Rose were somewhere among the watchers. He had asked them to come and see him off on his first trip. He was sure that Roxa and her family would be waiting to see them pass by Antiquity the following day.

As they reached the Point, they picked up the current from the Allegheny, and the combined currents of the two rivers helped push them onward into the Ohio, adding another four miles per hour to their own speed down the river. Tom took out his pocket watch and opened the lid. It was one o'clock, and he was hungry. He hadn't eaten a bite that day. He went to the cookhouse for a plate of stew, took out the *Alice Brown's* log book and crew roll to study and sat down at the dining table to eat his dinner. His first watch as mate would begin at four that afternoon. And, after three long years, he was finally free of standing those damned night watches. Three years, he thought later, as he went to his cabin, three long years of waiting for this … and for Roxa.

Tom woke to the sound of an insistent knocking on his door and the voice of the young watchman, "Four o'clock, sir." He hadn't meant to fall asleep, but he must have nodded off while studying the log book and trying to learn the names of the crew.

Mounting the stairs to the texas deck, he found Captain Leitz in the pilot house and greeted him, touching the brim of his cap. "Afternoon, Cap'n. Any orders for my watch, sir?"

"Get them deckhands of yours out on the tow, Tom, and have 'em check all the chains to make sure nothing has worked loose since we left Pittsburgh. We'll be passing Steubenville soon."

Tom found the two deckhands from his watch finishing mugs of coffee in the dining room and passed on the captain's orders to them. They were both young Irishmen, and one of them had a red beard that reminded him of Seamus Kelly. He thought briefly of his sister Mary with a pang of regret. Mary had changed after Seamus died. Part of her, her last hope of happiness, had died with him, leaving her a bitter, homebound spinster with two aging parents. Tom knew she was jealous of him and Pete, envying their freedom and happiness. He feared she would never leave the little house in East Bethlehem Township but would stay there the rest of her life, going to daily mass with Mam and helping her tend to Da while working hard as a seamstress to keep food on the table. In the latter role, she was not too proud to accept monthly checks from Pete and Rose, who were quite well off in Pittsburgh in spite of Pete's own excesses.

Troubled by these thoughts, he gladly went to work, leading the two Irish deckhands out onto the tow to check the rigging. Each of them carried a length of iron pipe with which they could apply extra leverage to the handles of the ratchets, taking up any slack in the rigging that had developed since leaving Pittsburgh. They walked gingerly along the narrow inboard gunwales of the two driver barges lashed on either side of the *Alice Brown's* wide bow, checking the tension of the rigging as they went toward the head of the tow.

The "duckpond," a large open gap ahead of the bow and surrounded on the other three sides by barges, was the most hazardous spot for the crew. Anything (or anybody) that dropped or fell into the churning water in the "duckpond" would be gone forever, sucked under and swept beneath the hull until caught by the big paddlewheel at the stern. Tom had once seen the mangled body of a young deckhand who had slipped on a wet gunwale and fallen into that boiling cauldron. Since then, he had always felt a tightening of his muscles as he passed forward on his way out to the tow.

Cholera. The mere word terrified most people. And it was waiting for the *Alice Brown* in New Orleans that year. News of the latest epidemic had traveled upriver with other boats. The crew learned from them that New Orleans' doctors and health officials had raised the alarm, with plans to prevent the spread of the disease by disinfecting and fumigating vessels, boarding houses, hotel rooms and the houses of victims. When they reached New Orleans at the end of April, Captain Leitz ordered the crew to remain on board for their own safety.

Only six years had passed since Tom had buried poor Seamus Kelly during the yellow fever epidemic of '67. The year before that, the last major cholera epidemic had swept through the land. Tom had no desire to risk catching the disease by going ashore in New Orleans. He would never forget what had happened to poor Seamus. It could just as easily be him lying in that grave in Memphis.

As the *Alice Brown* prepared to leave the city a few days later with a tow of empty barges, having delivered her cargo of coal, Tom was in charge of the boat as "officer of the deck" while the captain filed their manifest with the harbormaster. He could see the smoke of small fires rising above the levees, fires used to burn the bedding, clothing and personal belongings of the victims. Ordinary wagons driven by teamsters wearing masks to cover their faces were being used to collect some of the bodies, those of the poor and destitute, to be covered with quicklime and buried quickly in mass graves. In spite of such precautions, he knew that the cholera would probably continue to spread up the river to other cities, just as it had in '66, until it finally died out with the arrival of cold weather.

Suddenly he heard shouts from the wharf. Running to investigate the disturbance, he saw Big Ben, one of the *Alice Brown's* black stokers, struggling in the grip of two burly stevedores and a policeman. Ben had gone ashore the day before, disobeying Captain Leitz's express orders, and had spent the night somewhere in the city. Now, realizing too late his awful mistake, he was desperately trying to rejoin the boat and escape from the quarantine. Tom ran to the officers' gun locker and found a brand new Colt's Single Action .45. Returning to the deck and leveling the loaded pistol, he shouted, "Don't try it, Ben. My orders are to shoot anyone who tries to come aboard from the city, and I will shoot you, too, if I have to. You'll just have to take your chances with the rest. Good luck, Ben. I will pray that you'll still be here to join us again when the cholera's gone." The gun trembled in Tom's hand as he realized that what he was saying probably condemned the poor man to an even worse death.

Released by the three men, Ben slumped forward and covered his face with both hands. Without a word, shaking his head from side to side, he turned and walked slowly back into the city.

The rivers kept running high that spring, enabling the *Alice Brown* to make several more round trips to New Orleans. As they returned to Brown's Station at the end of May, Tom was weary of being continually confined aboard by the cholera quarantines in the cities along the river. He was looking forward to the return of low water, the end of the navigation season and spending the summer with Roxa on the farm. After the *Alice* was made fast to the Brown's wharf and secured for the night, Captain Leitz sent him to the office with the log book to report on their latest trip. To his delight, the night man handed him an envelope. "Letter from home, sir."

The envelope smelled faintly of lavender and was addressed in Roxa's rounded, precise schoolgirl script. He tore it open, allowing a tiny bunch of pressed violets to fall through his fingers. He read:

> *Antiquity, Ohio,*
> *May 15, 1873*
> *My dearest Husband,*
>
> *The spring rains are finally ending, and I am hoping the river will fall quickly and bring you home to me soon. After you left us last month, George fashioned a crude wooden flood gauge for me and planted it in the muddy river bottom below the house. I go there every morning, Tom, hoping to see a big drop in the water level. This morning the gauge was standing on dry land for the first time. I do believe the river has finally crested. My heart is filled with happiness, dearest, for I know you will be coming home to me soon.*
>
> *I have a special reason to want you here by my side, Tom. I believe I am expecting our first child...*

Tom stopped reading, overcome with joy. Everything in the little office suddenly seemed to glow with a warm light. He loved the whole world, wanted to hug the tired night man looking at him curiously across the counter. He heard the distant sound of a pool boat pushing a tow of loaded barges down the Mon from the mines to Pittsburgh. As it approached the tight bend at Brown's Station, the pilot blew a long blast on his whistle, warning any upriver traffic to make room for the tow to pass. The clear note reverberated through the gathering darkness from the high bluff behind the station. It was as if a heavenly brass ensemble had just sounded a fanfare, announcing the coming birth of their child.

He read on, his heart racing, but there was nothing more about this wonderful news. How typical of Roxa, he thought, simply to state it as a matter of fact and then go on to other subjects. She reported on the health of each of their family and friends. She wrote about the birth of a new calf and a litter of shoats. George was getting ready to do the spring plowing. The news of the cholera epidemic in New Orleans had reached Antiquity, but there were no cases there yet, and so on.

Folding the letter, he kissed it, put it in his shirt pocket next to his heart and turned again to the night man. "It's from my wife. She's expecting our first child." He smiled and went back on board to his cabin. He would be a father. But what kind of father would he be? Pray God, not one like his own father.

Low water was indeed late in coming that year, due to prolonged spring rains. Finally the Ohio began to recede in earnest, and by the end of July, Tom made his way home to Roxa, who was already showing her pregnancy.

During low water, when the men had all come home from the river, Brother Conyers' congregation joined forces to build a new, larger church to accommodate Antiquity's growing population, just a quarter of a mile upriver from the old church where they had been wed.

Chapter Eighteen

They named the baby Mary Catherine for Tom's youngest sister and the one member of his family he had always loved the best. She was born during a snow storm on Tuesday, December 16, 1873, exactly forty-one weeks after the wedding, and she weighed seven and a half pounds. Neighborhood busybodies carefully counted the weeks on their calendars, but there was no scandalous rumor for them to spread about the quiet Irish riverman who had waited so long to wed his village sweetheart.

The winter flood crest on the Ohio passed Antiquity the same day the baby was born, having risen more than forty feet in just two months, and Tom knew he must return to Brown's Station right after Christmas to rejoin his crew. Business was bad in Pittsburgh ever since the bank failures in New York in September. Pete had written that the iron works in Brady's Bend were laying off men and were on the verge of closing. Thousands of people were out of work, and the whole country seemed headed for a depression. He would do nothing to risk losing his own job, now that he and Roxa were responsible for another human life.

He had written to his parents to wish them a happy Christmas and to inform them about the birth of their first grandchild, but he had received no reply. His sister Katie had written back, though, thrilled by the news that her new niece had been named after her.

By the time the cholera had spread as far as Antiquity, winter had already arrived there, and only a few deaths occurred, mostly infants and elderly people. The school closed early for the holidays. Roxa and her family stayed at home to avoid exposure, not even going to church until Christmas day. After hearing the news of the terrible death toll in towns along the lower Ohio and in the slums of Cincinnati during the summer, Brother Conyers had advised his little flock to stay at home, read their Bibles and pray for God's deliverance.

The women in the family had all been sewing, knitting and crocheting during their enforced stays at home, and the fruits of their labors emerged, carefully wrapped in packages of brightly colored paper, in the Powells' kitchen on Christmas morning. Tom, George and Albert had store-bought presents for the ladies, acquired in their comings and goings to work. The elderly Varians, both now in their seventies, were home-bound in their neighboring house but eagerly awaited a first visit by Roxa and the baby, just nine days old. Roxa, too, was eager to get up after being kept in bed for more than a week.

A sudden cold snap gripped the Ohio Valley just before Christmas, and ice blocked the rivers near Pittsburgh for a week. An equally sudden thaw followed, and on Christmas Eve, the temperature reached an unseasonable seventy degrees. The next morning, Roxa came into the kitchen in her robe and slippers, walking carefully and hanging on to Tom's arm for support. She looked out the window at the column of mercury in the thermometer. "Mother, I think we can wrap Catherine up nice and warm in her new Christmas woolens and take her to visit Grandma and Grandpa for just a few minutes after church. I feel a lot stronger today, and it might do us all a lot of good to get out and breathe some fresh air. It's like a spring morning out there."

Almira Powell nodded. "If you really feel up to it, honey, by all means, let's go. Mother and Dad have been waiting to meet their new great-granddaughter for more than a week now." Having herself been born a middle child in a tough pioneer family of eight surviving siblings, she was never one to coddle either children or their parents.

Tom was delighted. He was so proud of Roxa and Catherine, he wanted the whole world to see them. He just hoped Catherine wouldn't wake up during the church service and start squalling. "Will Catherine be all right during worship, Roxa?"

Roxa laughed. "Don't worry, I'll give her my breast just before we go. She'll be sleeping like a top."

Thinking of Roxa's breasts, already beginning to swell with milk, Tom experienced a tingle between his legs that made him hot and flushed with embarrassment. They had abstained from lovemaking toward the end of her pregnancy and had not yet resumed it. He found himself fantasizing about her often, especially when she let him watch her nursing Catherine. Noticing his distraction, Roxa seemed to guess what was troubling him. "Why, Tom Malone, what on earth are you daydreaming about?" she asked teasingly.

"Nothing, Roxa. Nothing. I'll go and hitch up the horse."

George Walter Malone, Tom and Roxa's second child and first son, arrived on Wednesday, December 13, 1875, two years, almost to the day, after his sister Catherine, as if planned that way. He, too, was born during a snow storm. He weighed eight pounds. While both he and Roxa were happy to have a son, Tom noticed something different in Roxa's reaction to him, the way she held him and talked to him, as if some special bond existed between the two of them. Of course, she loved little Catherine too, her firstborn, but not the way she loved her son.

Folks in Antiquity, where life was dominated by the rise and fall of the river, jokingly remarked to Tom and Roxa on the similarities in the two birthdates, knowing how difficult it was for Tom to plan his visits to the farm during the busy navigation season. Roxa usually replied by quoting Tennyson's popular verse from *Locksley Hall*: "In the Spring a young man's fancy lightly turns to thoughts of love." Or sometimes, with really close friends, she would laugh and say, "I guess the sap was rising."

Tom admired Roxa's ability to come up with things to say on the spur of the moment. When people asked him questions, he was often at a loss to reply unless the question dealt with steam boating on the river or some other familiar topic. Roxa would usually come to his rescue and speak for him. He didn't mind at all when she did. He was happy to be off the hook and out of the limelight.

Chapter Nineteen: 1876

It was the year of the great Centennial, and Americans, finally recovering from the Panic of '73 and three long years of depression, were eager to celebrate the beginning of their second century of independence. Tom had come back from the river at the end of June, just in time to take Roxa, her mother and the two babies down to Pomeroy to watch the Fourth of July fireworks display on the Main Street riverfront. Catherine, two and a half years old, had not been frightened by the loud reports but had loved every minute, clapping her little hands along with the grownups after each big blossom of color, fire and noise against the night sky out over the Ohio.

After the grand finale had exploded in a volley of red, white and blue rockets and one extra loud bang, they found their way through the throngs of people, back up Court Street to the square by the courthouse on Second Street, where Tom had hitched the horse and buggy. The mare was nervous and skittish from the noisy fireworks, and Tom petted her to calm her down, holding her head and feeding her some oats while the two women climbed aboard with the little ones. On the way home, Tom thought about his trip to Alabama on the *Shark* in '64, the last time he had heard so many loud explosions. Those "fireworks" had not been intended to celebrate the Union, but rather to tear it apart. He had been terrified then, especially when he had seen the shot-riddled steamboat *Anna* drifting helplessly down the Tennessee River, her steam line severed by a Confederate cannon ball.

Tom had not seen his parents since their awful confrontation at Easter, three years earlier. He still received letters from Pete and his sisters, though, and he saw them occasionally. He would come up the river to Brownsville on a pool boat from time to time, picking up tows of loaded coalboats and barges, and when he did, Katie and Ellen would come across the river to the wharf to visit him, bringing the latest news of the "old folks". It hurt him that he could not even visit them after so long, but they were unrelenting – stubborn Ulster Catholics.

Then one afternoon on the Powell farm, a letter arrived from Pete: Their mother had died. She was only fifty-five, worn out by years of hard work and bearing eight children. Pete described the funeral at St. Peter's Church, attended by a large crowd of their friends from the Three Towns, where Margaret Malone had lived for the past thirty-four years. She had attended daily Mass at St. Peter's all those years, except when sickness or bad weather kept her at home.

Tom was thunderstruck. He felt an overwhelming sense of regret that he and Mam had never reconciled. And now they never would, never could. It was too late. Death had finished the job of separation that he himself had begun by leaving home so full of childish self-righteousness twelve years earlier on his birthday. How that must have hurt her. Nothing he could do or say now could ever undo the hurt he realized he had caused her then.

Folding the letter, Tom turned to Roxa, who held little George Walter in her arms. "She's dead, Roxa. Now she'll never get to know her grandchildren." Tears escaped from his eyes and gathered in his moustache as he shook his shaggy head. "I'm going back there as soon as the river's high enough. Maybe Da will let me come to visit him. At least I can go to Mam's grave and say a prayer for her."

"We'll all pray for her here in Antiquity too, Tom." Roxa reached out to him with her free hand and touched his bearded, weather-beaten cheek. "The Lord will surely forgive her for hurting you so much."

Tom left the *Alice Brown* in Pittsburgh preparing for her first trip downriver in the new fall navigation season. He caught a ride up the Monongahela on one of the Brown's Line pool boats, which were busily plying back and forth from the Alicia Mines to the Pittsburgh Harbor, assembling tows of loaded barges and coalboats for the bigger towboats to take on down the river. The maples on the hills were already aflame with fall colors as they arrived at the wharf in Brownsville. It had been just such a glorious fall day twelve years earlier on his eighteenth birthday, when he had left home, haunted by memories of his beating, to begin his career on the river. Each homecoming after that had been full of pain and regret, and this one was no exception.

"I'm going ashore for a little while, Captain. Got to visit my mother. I'll be back before dark." He put on his mate's cap and left the wheelhouse. The little flower shop on Front Street was still open, selling the last summer roses. Roses were her favorite, he thought. Tom bought a bunch of them and trudged up the steep hill past Nemacolin Castle and on up Market Street toward St. Peter's Catholic Church.

He remembered the day of his First Communion, twenty-four years before, when he and his mother had climbed this same hill together. That time he had been clutching her hand tightly with his own small one, his mind full of fears that something terrible might happen to him when he ate the body and blood of Jesus. What would happen when he had to let go of her hand and meet the priest at the altar? He would be alone. He looked up at her walking beside him. "Mam, couldn't you go up to the altar with me fer the communion? Please, Mam?"

"Now, Tommy, don't ye be silly. The other wee ones will not be hanging on their mammies, now will they? Don't ye be making us ashamed o' ye in front of Father the now. Do be a brave lad and make us proud o' ye." From that moment on he had tried to make both of them proud of him. He wondered, though, if he had ever really succeeded.

Finally, he reached the top of the steps leading up to the churchyard and looked for his mother's grave. Finding it, he approached, gently laid the roses down and knelt to pray. Since his marriage to Roxa he had faithfully worshiped at the little Baptist church in Antiquity every summer Sunday during low water season. But, when Tom prayed, he still used the words he had learned as a boy, and so he now began with the *Hail, Mary*, whispering softly under his breath, and ending with "pray for us sinners now and at the hour of our death. Amen."

After crossing himself in the old way, he rose and started back down the hill. He paused once at the top of the steep steps leading from the churchyard down to the street. Turning for one more look, he saw the gray stone façade of the church towering above his mother's grave, stones his father had helped to heave into place the year before he was born.

He would not go across the river to see his father.

Epilogue

Tom loved his work and the responsibility of being second in command on a great towboat, but he knew the time had come for him to leave the river and look for a job on land in a place where the children could attend a better school than Aunt Jenny's one-room schoolhouse in Antiquity. Tom finally resigned his job as mate in 1880 and got a job at Brown's Station as a watchman. The Malones moved from the Powell farm in Antiquity to a little company-owned house on Second Avenue between the B&O railroad tracks and the river, within easy walking distance of the Browns' coal yard.

Although Tom continued to work as a watchman at Brown's Station for three more years, the family soon moved to a larger house on Lytle Street in Hazelwood to be closer to the church and the children's school. In June of 1883, Tom and Roxa had another daughter. They named the baby Almira Powell Malone after Roxa's mother and called her "Alma." Tom decided to look for another job. Brown's Station was a longer hike from their new home in the center of town. Each weekday for three years, as Tom walked the three miles to work along Second Avenue, he passed the busy B&O freight yard in Glenwood. Then, the same summer Alma was born, the B&O built a new roundhouse and locomotive repair shop only a half-mile away, down at the foot of Lytle Street. Tom applied for a job there and was accepted immediately at a higher wage than he could possibly earn at

Brown's Station. With mixed feelings, he gave Brown's Line his notice and ended his nineteen-year career as a riverman.

Then began the happiest years of Tom's life. He was thirty-seven; in perfect health; happily married to the one true love of his life; father of three healthy, bright children; holding down a good, steady job and still keeping in touch with his former coalboating comrades when they came to Pittsburgh Harbor or Brown's Station.

Tom's father, Jack Malone, died in 1887 in the little house in East Bethlehem, attended in his final illness by Mary, who had faithfully kept house and cared for the old man following her mother's death. Tom continued to visit Katie in Brownsville until her death in 1932, but he never visited Mary. In 1893, George Powell and his family moved from Antiquity to Pittsburgh too, and George went to work with Tom at the Glenwood Locomotive Shop.

Catherine and Walter were both married on consecutive days in June, 1902. Walter married a quiet, serious Irish girl, Emily Moses, from County Tyrone. Soon there were grandchildren, including my father, another Jack Malone, born on the first of July, 1903.

Tom's brother Pete had fallen upon hard times and was still drinking heavily. Tom helped Rose care for him and paid some of his debts. Pete died in March 1910, followed only three months later by poor, long-suffering Rose, who never stopped loving him.

Tom, Roxa and Alma moved from Lytle Street to a smaller house on Trenton Avenue in Glenwood, even closer to Tom's work in the Glenwood shops. In 1913, Alma got married and went to live on a farm in Lake County, Ohio. That same year Tom retired from the B&O Railroad after thirty years of service. He was sixty-seven, still hale and hearty.

After Tom retired, he and Roxa spent several summers back on the Powell farm in Antiquity, surrounded by old friends and relatives. Tom loved to fix things on the farm and always kept his tools clean and sharp. They kept in regular touch with their children and grandchildren back in Pittsburgh while they were away.

They sold the house on Trenton Avenue and moved to Crafton to be near Walter and also to Catherine, whose husband, Tom Anderson had died in 1915. In the fall of 1917, Roxa's mother was beginning to fail after many years of perfect good health. They went down to Antiquity to take care of her, but on December 7, after trying to move her heavy, cast iron cook stove a few feet by herself, Almira Varian "Granny" Powell died on her kitchen floor of a heart attack, aged eighty-seven.

Starting in 1919, Tom and Roxa spent every summer with their daughter Alma and her husband on their farm in Ohio. Then, in 1925, Roxa was not feeling well, and they returned earlier than usual from Ohio. Suddenly, on September first, a massive stroke ended Roxa's life in a few hours. Tom was stunned. He sat silent and mute. He never did say much; Roxa had always been the talkative one of the two. He never made a fuss about anything, or even raised his voice when any of his grandchildren got out of line.

Tom spent the rest of his life living with Catherine in Crafton. There, he fell into a sort of routine: for instance, on Mondays he liked to take a street car into the city in the morning, to walk along the river, to look at the boats and, especially, to go aboard any that happened to be at the wharf. After lunch at one of the restaurants near the Old Market House, he would see a movie or, what he liked best of all, a vaudeville show at the Harris Theater. Trained dogs and trapeze artists were his favorites. Before taking the street car back to Catherine's house in Crafton he would often stop for a few minutes to visit Walter at his office on Third Avenue. On these weekly excursions, Tom always carried all of his money in a big roll secured by a rubber band. This worried Catherine, who was afraid that some of the seedy characters around the wharf or the Diamond Street saloons would waylay the old man and perhaps injure him if they saw his money.

More tragedy invaded Tom's quiet life with the death of his grandson, Tom Anderson, Jr., on September 9, 1931, followed in less than two years by the death of his only son, Walter Malone, on June 30, 1933. After that he seemed to be more and more withdrawn from life. He liked to retire to his room in Catherine's house to read the newspapers and novels about outdoor life. Zane Gray was one of his favorites.

Tom was a very religious man. Though a Protestant convert, he never ate meat on Fridays, still faithfully keeping a promise he made to his mother before he left Brownsville to work on the river in 1864. All the rest of his life, after he met Roxa, he went to church regularly and, for a number of years, was a member of a men's Bible class.

After a life of almost perfect health, Thomas James Malone, my great-grandfather, succumbed to an acute kidney infection on May 9, 1936, just a few months short of his ninetieth birthday.

John Malone

Envoi

Under the wide and starry sky
Dig the grave, and let me lie.
Glad did I live, and gladly die,
                    And I laid me down with a will.
This be the verse you grave for me:
Here he lies where he longed to be;
Home is the sailor, home from the sea,
                    And the hunter home from the hill.

—Robert Louis Stevenson, *"Requiem"*, 1880

www.ingramcontent.com/pod-product-compliance
Lightning Source LLC
Chambersburg PA
CBHW020624250626
47154CB00004B/1662